The Cursed Scion
of
Kuru

Maharudra Chakraborty

JOLPIC MAGAZINE PUBLICATION

The Cursed Scion of Kuru

A Philosophical Fantasy Thriller Novel

Maharudra Chakraborty asserts the moral right to be identified as the author of this book.
Email id of the author: cmaharudra@gmail.com

First Published in 2021
ISBN: 9798782836856

JOLPIC MAGAZINE PUBLICATION

Dedicated to all good souls...

Preface

This novel has been written for people of all ages, to read. Children can read this novel as a storybook, and they gather knowledge about moral values in their lives through their subconscious mind, which will help them to build a good character for the future. On the other hand, adults are able to conceive the deeper meaning of life through this novel.

It is not merely a fantasy or thriller novel, which people generally read for their entertainment. It is a novel about the meaning of life, and regarding the psychology of an individual. What would a person do if he suddenly lost everything in his life? His entire wealth, his recognition, his family, his friends, and everything that he had possessed once, except his memory. Would he choose death? Or, should he begin his life with a new ambition? How can an evil force take away everything from someone's life? How should the person defeat that force leading a good life?

This novel answers all these questions through its story. And moreover, it delivers the basic knowledge of Hinduism among the readers.

Contents

Chapter One

The sparrow with its missing tail

On a nice morning, the young prince came out from his bedroom, and stepped to the balcony, from where the snow covered mountains could be clearly seen. He looked at the mountains, and inhaled some fresh air pouring into his lungs. Winter had not yet gone away, the prince felt it, as the cold wind shivered him a little. His reflex compelled him to draw the fur coat more tightly on his body. But at the very next moment, his facial expression changed. It seemed that a sudden anger overpowered him, and had taken away all of his happiness that he possessed.

He thought about something for a while, and then he removed the fur coat from his body and threw it on the balcony floor. He began to feel the cold. He tried to enhance his ability of tolerance against the chilling sensation. But the cold wind, which was coming from the north, did not let him stay uncovered. He picked up the coat from the floor, and wrapped it on his body again.

That day was his birthday. He became eighteen, and it was the age of entering adulthood according to the rule made by ancient kings of the dynasty, in which he belonged. If he became an adult, he should have the ability to endure the cold. But nothing had changed - he thought.

He went back to the room and saw his face in a large mirror that was fitted on a table. He examined his eyes, his nose, his lips, his cheeks, his ears, his biceps and other parts of his body. There was no change, he found.

Then what could be the meaning of adulthood, he asked himself. Disappointed prince sat on his bed, which was placed at the center of the room. Then he looked at the walls. Several hand drawn pictures of his forefathers were hanging there. Twenty pictures were there including his grandfather and father. All of them had served as the kings in his kingdom, and had grown the kingdom greater and more prosperous, except his grandfather and father. He knew well that neither his grandfather nor his father had fought any battle to conquer the neighboring kingdom, to extend the area of the land from its present boundaries.

Along with those ancient kings, there was one larger picture on the wall. It was an entire map of the kingdom, depicting all the boundaries of it; the great kingdom of Kuru.

His eyes stuck to the map. He carefully examined it. The boundaries clearly made a picture of a sparrow; the prince suddenly found. But, where was its tail? How could a bird survive without its tail? The map was not complete yet; it still needed the remaining portion of its body to show its completeness. He stared at the boundary to find out the tail, and finally he found indeed. There was a small neighboring kingdom of Kuru, called Anga, that would complete the full body of the sparrow. Boundary lines of Anga were exactly making a figure of the sparrow's tail.

He needed Anga badly, he vowed.

A sound of approaching footsteps outside of the entrance door distracted him from the thoughts. Someone was coming to his room. He had predicted that the person might be his father, but soon he realized that it was someone else, as he heard the voice of one of the royal servants.

"The emperor of Kuru, the great Mahendra, wants to meet you, your royal highness. He's waiting for your consent to enter."

The prince wondered for a while. If his father wanted to meet him, he was allowed to meet him anytime. Why would he send any servant? He asked many questions himself, as he experienced such an unusual behavior from his father for the first time.

Finding no explanation, he walked to the door to open, after getting up from the bed, and found his father was standing beside the servant, who was carrying a large copper plate containing various flowers, a curdy paste of sandalwood, an earthen lamp, and other various sacred substances. The prince realized that the king came to bless him for the future on his eighteenth birthday performing a sacred ritual, which he always did on his every birthday.

Many years ago, when he was a baby, his mother died after suffering from an incurable disease. Still, the emperor did not let his son feel any deficiency of a mother. He provided his son with all the extent of love that he was capable of. If the king Mahendra wanted to be married once more, and presented his son a step mother, he was free to do that. But, he did not marry again, as he was concerned about the future of his son.

Who could guarantee that the new wedded queen would not put a condition that her son would have to be the future king, in the place of his present son? Maybe, her beauty would obsess the emperor in a state that he would not have any option, but to obey her.

Many hundreds of years ago, one of his forefathers, the great emperor of Kuru dynasty, king Santanu had married for the second time, as his first wife, Ganga, refused to stay with him, and left him forever. And that marriage implemented the first root of the great war, the war of Kurukshetra. King Santanu's two branches of descendants Kaurava and Pandava had shown enmity against each other forgetting their brotherhood. And the final battle of Kurukshetra had ended with many tragedies. The battle took away many lives. Even no heir was alive of the victorious Pandavas, except Parikshit. He was the grandson of Arjuna. The emperor Mahendra was the present heir of Parikshit, he knew it. The entire history of Kurukshetra war had been written in a sacred book called Mahabharata. He had read the book many years ago, and he was deeply concerned about the future that he would not allow the bloody history to be repeated again.

The prince opened the door and saw his father greeted him with a wide smile. The prince also delivered a smile in return and welcomed him inside.

"Happy birthday dear son."

Mahendra began the ritualistic procedure. He picked up some flowers from the plate, and showered over his head. And then he took the lamp and moved before the prince in a circular motion and, after performing other rituals, at the end, the emperor Mahendra made a sacred symbol on his forehead with sandalwood paste. During the entire ritual, the prince bowed down silent with his hands folded in the praying gesture. Then Mahendra placed his palms on his head to bless him and said, "Dear Aditya, the heir of the great warrior Arjuna, may god provide you all the abilities that Arjuna possessed. May god make you as bright as the sun that the brightness of your glory will spread throughout every corner of the world. I pray to god for your prosperity and good future."

Mahendra paused for a while, then said, "And now is the time to reveal the gift for you on your eighteenth birthday."

"Anything special?" asked Aditya in surprise.

"Obviously my son."

Mahendra waved his hand to the servant, instructing him to fetch the gift. The servant left the room following the emperor's instruction. Prince Aditya got the chance to ask the question that he was looking for, and he asked, "Pitasree (father), I couldn't understand why you waited outside today and asked for my consent to enter the room. I've never experienced such etiquette from you. You always came to my room anytime you wanted, even yesterday was the same. What is the reason for the recent alteration?"

"Because you became an adult today. According to the rule of Kuru, the eighteen-year age is the threshold of entering adulthood. As you completed eighteen years today, you are considered to be a mature person, and from today everyone will respect you, just like I get respect from everyone. There will be no exception also from me. From today, I'll always ask for your consent in a few matters, which are related to your basic rights," clarified Mahendra.

Aditya got disappointed as he had expected more. He just mumbled, "That is what adulthood means?"

"It seems you are not very satisfied availing the advantage of adulthood," said the emperor.

"I expected more," sighed Aditya.

"Hmm. There are more advantages when someone becomes an adult. You've not to worry."

Aditya was going to say something, but at that moment, the servant brought the present. It was a sword. The intensity of disappointment in Aditya increased further, as he did not like the gift. He already owned many swords of various shapes and sizes, and that new sword would merely increase the number. He failed to suppress his dissatisfaction, and he sighed, "It's just a sword."

Mahendra took the sword from the servant and opened it from the scabbard to show it to Aditya. The neatly polished blade reflected light like a mirror.

"It's not an ordinary sword dear. It is the most expensive sword that has been ever made. It has been delivered here today's morning, having travelled a long distance from Gandhar. Its blade has been manufactured by the renowned blacksmiths of Gandhar, and its hilt is made of gold. Take a look at it closely. See, how these precious gems on its hilt have enhanced its beauty."

Then he balanced the sword on a finger and said, "See, its balance. It'll assist you to get extra momentum while swiping. And the most important feature of this expensive sword is that the sharpness of its edge will never decrease."

Still, Aditya did not show happiness. He took the sword from father's hand and said, "Where should I use this thing? It has no use, Pitasree."

"Not necessarily you've used everything that you've owned. Consider this sword as a precious collection, and preserve it."

"This precious collection could not satisfy me. I want to collect something more precious."

"What is your expectation, son? I want to see you always happy, and if I am able to afford the thing, which you want, obviously I can manage it for you," said the emperor.

"Certainly you can. It's not very difficult to afford."

"Just let me know about your need, my son. I'll definitely purchase the thing for you," said Mahendra, gleaming his face.

"It cannot be purchased, Pitasree."

"Then?"

"It has to be taken away. It's only the tail of a sparrow that is still missing from the sparrow's body."

"I couldn't understand what you're saying."

Suddenly the voice of the prince became firm and his face was expressing cruelty, and he pointed the tip of that expensive sword to the picture, which was depicting the map of Kuru kingdom. He said, "Look at our boundaries, it's perfectly making a figure of a sparrow. But its tail is missing. I want its tail to complete its body."

Mahendra carefully looked at the map, and became stunned after extracting the meaning of Aditya's abstract talking. His face became rigid, and some spontaneous words came out from his mouth, "Anga? Impossible!"

"It's certainly possible through a minor battle."

The servant was standing there. Mahendra ordered him to leave them alone, and the servant left the room. Then Mahendra said to Aditya, "You've no idea what you are demanding."

"Anga is a small province. We can easily conquer the kingdom, deploying only one tenth of our soldiers."

"It's not about any battle. I'm talking about morality. Kuru has a friendly relationship of more than thousand years with Anga," clarified Mahendra.

"I think, there will be no problem for us, if we break friendship with that tiny province."

"Did you forget the history? Many years ago Duryadhan gifted the province to his intimate friend Karna. And morality taught us that a gifted thing should not be taken back from someone," scolded Mahendra.

"Pitasree, Duryadhan and Karna, both of them do not exist in recent days. And if you carefully search about our history, you'll find those two evil persons were the greatest enemies of our ancestor, Arjuna. So, there will be no question of immorality, if we conquer Anga."

"But, in the later stage, Pandavas' family became friends with Karna's family. And that relation still exists today."

"We can break the friendship," said Aditya.

"But Anga's king, Samhati, and I are good friends till today."

"A friendship can be broken, if a father loves his son more than his friend."

Mahendra sighed, but did not reply. He was deeply thinking about something, leaning his head downward.

Aditya did not stop his speaking. He said pointing to the pictures of previous emperors, "See our forefathers. They had fought many battles in their times, and conquered several smaller provinces. That was the way how our Kuru had grown, and became prosperous to its present state. Maybe, kings of those provinces had had good relations with them, yet our forefathers did not show reluctance to fight any battle. We should follow the same path that our forefathers had followed."

After a long pause, Mahendra finally declared, "Your wish will be fulfilled. Anga will be ours very soon. We are going to invade Anga, and the extended territory of Kuru will be declared after the battle."

Mahendra left the room without speaking further, but he was not pleased announcing the declaration to Aditya. His face became firm, and smile had gone away.

However, Aditya was smiling, as he was imagining the new map of Kuru kingdom inside his mind.

Chapter Two

The curse

Sand and Dust covered the surroundings, as thousands of the soldiers marched across the border of Kuru, and trespassed on the land of Anga. Most of the soldiers were marching on their feet, and many were mounted on horses and elephants. The leading position of the troops contained chariots of different sizes. Every chariot was drawn by four to five horses, and the charioteer, sitting on the front, was leading the chariot managing the paces of those horses. Two of the chariots were enormous and magnificently decorated. Those were assigned for the emperor of Kuru, Mahendra, and his son, Aditya. Flags of Kuru kingdom were fluttering on the top of the chariots, and infantrymen were also carrying the same flags attached on long wooden sticks.

Having travelled a few miles from the border of Anga, the troops halted in a deserted ground beside a hilly area, as they saw the opponent soldiers were ready to defend Anga kingdom from the invaders.

Aditya tried to estimate their number, and realized that defeating all of them would not be a very hard task for Kuru's soldiers. He said to his father with excitement, "Pitasree, it seems we've brought more than enough men. If we deploy less than half of the soldiers here, we can easily win the battle like a finger snap."

"They have not attacked us yet. I can't understand what their plan is."

"Maybe they're thinking for the surrender," laughed Aditya.

"I don't think so. As far as I know about Samhati, he is not that kind of person who'll surrender to the enemy before showing his courage. He'll definitely fight."

"Look Pitasree (father)! two horse riders are coming toward us along with a small group of soldiers. What is their plan? We should command our army to attack them."

"Wait. They're not coming to attack us. They want to talk. One of them is Samhati himself, and the other one is his son, Vikarna."

Aditya looked again at them to recognize their faces, and indeed Samhati was coming towards them along with his son. They were carrying weapons, he found. Then, they were not coming to surrender, but wanted to make a deal, Aditya predicted. What could it be?

Soon they came closer and halted at a safe distance surrounded by Anga's soldiers. Samhati began to speak.

"I always thought that Kuru is a peace loving country, and it would never desire to conquer its neighbouring provinces. But, I was wrong. Anga has been performing its duty as a friendly province, and has paid taxes to Kuru during many centuries. But you broke that treaty, and came here to invade our land! Your forefathers would be ashamed of seeing your actions, if they were alive today."

"I am the emperor of Kuru, and you have no authority to teach me what is right and what is wrong. My son has wished on his eighteenth birthday that Kuru should declare its new border encompassing Anga province. As a father, it's my primary duty to keep my son happy, and I'm merely doing my duty," said Mahendra.

"You're speaking like the ancient king, Dhritarashtra who never considered the sins of his son Duryadhan to be judged, and day after day, Duryadhan became a person of evil qualities. At the end, there was an inevitable war, the great battle of Kurukshetra. It had taken many lives, and entire humanity was at risk. You're going to do the same kind of action right now. You came here with this huge group of trained soldiers, and kill our insufficient number of army to fulfil an insane demand of your son! You've lost all the moral values that your dynasty had possessed for years, and now you became thirsty for blood, like a monster," scolded Samhati.

"Listen Samhati, according to the rule made by the ancient kings, invasion of other's province is not a sin, and every invasion follows a war. Spilling of blood is an unavoidable result of a war. There is no way of achieving victory in a war without bloodshed. However, the war can be avoided if you surrender along with your soldiers. I can assure you that all of you will be treated well under the guidance of Kuru."

"No, Never. It's my duty to protect my land, and as long as I'm alive, no one has the power to take this land away from me," said Samhati.

"Then prepare your army· for the battle. No way remained to stop the bloodshed."

At that moment, Samhati's face changed suddenly. A brightness of hope was seen in his appearance. It seemed that he was waiting for that direction of the conversation. Aditya noticed that change.

Samhati said, "Still, there is a way by which we can save the lives of all soldiers."

"How?" asked Mahendra.

"Fighting a duel."

"Duel?"

"Yes. A duel can save many lives. You fight against me with your sword. And after killing me, Anga will be yours. It will save all these soldiers' lives, but will take only mine."

Mahendra was going to say something, but before he could say, Aditya shouted to warn his father, "Do not agree, Pitasree. He might have a dreadful plan against you. Be careful before falling into the trap of his words."

Samhati laughed at them, "What's the matter, Mahendra? The great emperor of Kuru is afraid of fighting a duel against an ordinary king! Remember Mahendra, you may reject the proposal of a duel, and achieve a mischievous victory deploying all these soldiers. But, people will gossip about you for many years, because of your spineless activity that you refused to fight a duel during a war against your enemy due to fear of death."

"Stop all these insulting statements now!" said Mahendra angrily, "I'm ready to fight against you alone, and at the end you will be decapitated by my sword."

Mahendra got down from his chariot carrying a sword along with a shield and approached Samhati. On the other hand, Samhati stepped forward to fight, and the duel began.

As the first sound of clashing of swords reached the ears of soldiers, they began to cheer their respective lieges. Both of the rulers were equally strong and well trained in sword fighting, thus there was no way to predict who would be the winner until the battle ended. Aditya's face became firm and tensed thinking of the present situation, as it did not go the same that he expected while he had aimed the invasion of Anga. Although the plan did not match his expectation, he was quite sure that his father would defeat Samhati effortlessly. But Samhati's good weapon skills made him apprehensive.

He turned his eyes from the ongoing duel, and glanced at Vikarna's face. He just wanted to know how his face reacted when his father engaged in the battle. It would make a relief in Aditya's mind if he could have seen the same kind of reaction on Vikarna's face that Aditya was suffering with.

Aditya had a strange mentality from his childhood that whenever he felt upset for any trivial reason, he searched a random person, and tortured the person until he cried. Most of the time he chose one of his friends who had a weaker physique than Aditya. It would be easier for him to torture. When his prey began crying, he felt a mental pleasure for some unknown reason. Being a prince, no one had ever dared to stop Aditya from doing such a brutal game. As he became an adult, he continued it, and day by day he was becoming an evil. His father had been aware of all the atrocities that Aditya had been committing for years, yet king Mahendra did not resist him ever.

Being the father of a motherless kid, Mahendra was sympathetic to his son, and he had taken care of a good father-son relationship during any casual conversation with Aditya. To maintain such empathic behavior, he overlooked many offences of Aditya since his childhood, and the result was undesirable. Aditya had taken the entire advantages of his freedom that he acquired from his father, thus he was able to do any sinful act that he wanted to do.

Mahendra presumed that the mentality of his son would change with time. When he would be mature enough to understand the moral ethics of a human being, automatically it would take an effect on his behavioral development. But, over the course of time, nothing had changed. As he grew up, ruthlessness in his behavior became more explicit.

Mahendra had tried to change Aditya's mentality on a later stage, but he failed. Morality can only be taught to a person from his premature state of mind. Otherwise, it would be impossible to change someone's mentality, unless the person encounters an extreme distressful situation in his life.

The duel was going on, and along with that a similar kind of storm inside of Vikarna's mind was also going on. Aditya noticed the mental condition of his enemy taking a quick glance at his face. It gave him a little relief from the tremendous amount of stress. At that anxious state of his mind, there was no other possible way to provide some comfort to Aditya except when his enemy was also in a trouble. He continued to watch the fight again, consoling himself that his father would definitely win the fight and conquer Anga.

Soon the duel was becoming hard to win for Anga, as Samhati seemed to have fallen tired continuing the fight for longer. Droplets of sweat were shining on his forehead, and he was compelled to step back for several instances to save himself from the deadly blows of Mahendra's blade. Aditya's face gleamed with the certainty of Kuru's victory. His wish was going to be fulfilled at last. The sparrow would avail its tail soon after the conclusion of the fight.

But, sometimes the most unfortunate incident happens when the situation goes in somebody's extreme favor. A great disappointment waited for Aditya.

Aditya's predictive mind was telling that Samhati was about to lose the fight, and his father would declare the vanquishment of Anga just after killing Samhati by his undefeatable skill of sword. But, at the very next moment when his expectation reached its peak, an almost devastated Samhati regained his power from the indomitable wish of saving Anga from outsiders. Suddenly he began to slash his blade in such a random way that the techniques of the movement of his sword could not be found in any guidelines of sword fighting. Mahendra was continuously stepping back to avoid the deadly blows from Samhati's sword. It seemed that at any moment Samhati's sword was able to make a severe wound on Mahendra's body.

Aditya's face became stiffened again and wrinkles appeared on his forehead observing the sudden reversal of the duel. He looked again at Vikarna, and saw he was with a smiling face, that made him more uncomfortable than ever. He could not find a suitable way to help his father in the duel. If a duel allowed a third person to interfere, he would have definitely cut off Samhati's head from the rest of his body.

The incident that happened next was completely uncertain for anyone, who were present in the battlefield. Samhati was swiping his sword like an insane and Mahendra was continuously leaping on the ground and leaning down his head to get escape from the sharp edge of Samhati's sword as his own sword was not enough to resist the faster blade swiping of Samhati. One moment came when the swiping of Samhati's sword was so deadly that Mahendra managed to save himself from the blow leaping higher, and when he landed back, he failed to keep on his balance properly, and his sword was detached from his hand as soon as his torso touched the ground.

It was quite an embarrassing situation for Mahendra. Being an emperor of Kuru and heir of the greatest warrior Arjuna, he should likely win a duel against other minor kings like Samhati. But the actual incident was entirely different.

There was a pin drop silence among the Kuru's army, as they saw their ruler lying on the ground unarmed.

The emperor of Kuru, Mahendra the great, sat on the ground perplexed by his own inability to defeat Samhati, and his sword was lying abandoned, a few feet away from his position. The sudden bafflement did not let him pick up the sword quickly, and to fight back again. He remained unarmed and looked at Samhati's face in bewilderment, forgetting the fear of upcoming death.

On the other hand, Samhati hurried towards him, raising his sword. Finally, he got a remarkable opportunity to save his land, and if he lost the opportunity at that moment, it would never return. But he could not accomplish the desired task. Before he could stab the sword on Mahendra's chest, an arrow was shot from elsewhere, and penetrated Samhati's body.

Samhati fell on the ground instantly, gasping heavily in tremendous pain. He wanted to speak something, but when he opened his mouth to speak, plenty of blood came out from there. Surely the arrow had penetrated his heart.

Vikarna took a few moments to realize that his father was wounded somehow, and when he realized, he cried out, "Father!" and he rushed towards Samhati.

All the soldiers of Kuru looked around to find out the person who had shot the opponent king down, but they could not see anyone among them who had a dare to shoot an arrow during an ongoing duel.

Mahendra looked at his son and saw Aditya was standing on his chariot holding a bow. His face along with his eyes became red in anger, and his chest was moving up and down due to heavy breathing just like a lion hunted its desired prey.

Mahendra whispered some words to him, "Son, why did you do that?" but there was no way, through which those words could reach Aditya's ears.

"They've tricked us. Tell our soldiers to attack," shouted Vikarna with moistened eyes. And finally the unavoidable battle began.

*****

Just before the end of the day, Kuru achieved victory in that battle. Every single soldier of Anga was dead. It happened because of Aditya. He had instructed Kuru's soldiers to kill all the opponent soldiers mercilessly, without giving them any chance to fight back. Thus those, who wanted to retreat away from the battleground or to surrender, had been killed by Kuru's army.

The sun had set a few moments ago, and the western sky was still red as blood. There was more red color on the battleground as an uncountable number of soldiers' dead bodies were lying on the ground covered with extreme blood.

"So, you were dreaming of conquering the kingdom of Kuru, isn't it?" asked Aditya in a sharp and loud voice.

Vikarna was kneeling down in the midst of the battlefield, and Aditya gently nudged the sharp point of his sword on Vikarna's chest. It was that sword which had been gifted by his father on his eighteenth birthday.

Aditya could have killed Vikarna at any point of time, but he wanted to play with him before taking his life away, just like a ferocious lion plays with its prey before making into a food. Vikarna was badly wounded due to weapon strikes, and many spots of his body were covered with fresh blood. His hands had been tied in his back so he was helpless to defend himself. Hundreds of falcons were flying around above the battleground, as there were plenty of foods available for them as dead bodies of soldiers.

Vikarna did not reply to Aditya and remained silent facing downwards. It caused more anger inside Aditya. He pressed the sword a little harder on Vikarna's chest. Vikarna felt the severe pain, and blood came out, yet he did not yell to express it. He was enduring everything, still his deformed face was showing that he was suffering badly.

"Speak out Vikarna, why were you greedy about Kuru?" asked Aditya again.

"Ha... Ha... Ha... Ha..."

Suddenly Vikarna broke out with a pointless laugh. It gave Aditya a cold shock of fear through his spine. How could a person laugh that way, when he knew his death was near? Aditya asked himself.

"Do you always blame others for your own faults?" asked Vikarna with a blood stained smiling face.

"What do you mean?"

"You have broken the treaty between Kuru and Anga, and taken our land forcefully despite having enough land of yours. Now you're blaming us that we are greedy?"

"There would be no need for a war, if you offered the land peacefully to us. But you didn't do the same."

"Anga belonged to us, and it's our utmost duty to protect our land and our people from invaders."

"Probably you forgot, this land Anga once belonged to Kuru. It was merely the generosity of my forefather that he gifted the land to you. I wanted to take the land back."

"Gifted things should not be taken away," cried out Vikarna.

"I needed Anga, as I need air to survive. Thus we did exactly what we were supposed to do," said Aditya.

"But, you killed my father unlawfully. You shot him when he was involved in a duel. It's against the rule of any war. Not only that, you killed all of my soldiers, even those who wanted to retreat away or surrender to save themselves. You've committed several heinous crimes one after one, and for that reason, there will be no mercy for you. Stay prepared for the punishment."

"How hilarious this is," laughed Aditya, "A poor prince of a subordinate land is threatening me for my feat! Probably he has forgotten that he is sitting at the edge of my sword, and at any point of time, his life will be ended."

Sighed Vikarna, and inhaled lots of air as much as he could, and said, staring at Aditya narrowing his eyes, "A

Kshatriya should not have a fear of death. Being a Kshatriya, I do not have any fear of dying; you are free to kill me whenever you want, but you deserve a severe punishment for your sins. And in the name of my father's soul, I put a curse on you that you will lose everything that you possess right now. You will lose Kuru along with this land Anga. Your identity as a prince will be lost along with all the comforts that you've entertained as a prince. The castle where you lived from your childhood, will not remain your home anymore. Emperor Mahendra, whom you know as your father, will refuse to recognize you..."

Vikarna could not finish his speech. Before he could, Aditya swiftly moved his sword across Vikarna's neck, and within a blink of eyes, Vikarna's severed head fell on the ground.

Those words, which were coming out from Vikarna's lips, were penetrating Aditya's ears with like thousands of swords. When Vikarna had mentioned his father's name, Aditya was unable to stay stagnant.

Mahendra was standing there and listening to the entire conversation that had been going on between Vikarna and his son. The ongoing situation could have been different if Mahendra interacted with Vikarna instead of Aditya. But an inexplicable force was acting on him all the time, and that force had compelled him to stay inert during the conversation. Possibly that force had originated from Aditya's arrogance, as he feared that any interference might have made Aditya angrier than ever, which no one could imagine.

Aditya threw a cruel smile at the severed head of Vikarna, and wiped the blood stained sword with a piece of cloth tearing from his own dress. Then he looked at the sky and took a deep breath of satisfaction, closing his eyes. Ultimately Anga had been conquered.

Aditya expressed happiness to his father, smiling at him. Mahendra smiled back, but there was a little dullness in that smile. Aditya noticed that his father was not happy at all, after achieving the victory.

He curiously asked, "It seems you're not cheerful enough. What's the matter, Pitashree (father)?"

"No, it's alright," answered Mahendra.

"Still pitashree, your face is not glowing like always. It glows whenever you feel happy. Rather at present it looks pale, as if some kind of deep sorrow has taken away all your happiness. Please let me know, Pitashree, what the reason for your dissatisfaction is."

Mahendra sighed, "Dear son, what we have achieved today, is not called a victory. Instead, you may call it a robbery."

"Why father? Why are you thinking so? Didn't you see how I managed to kill Samhati at the right moment when he was about to take your life? We didn't spare him along with his son, and the rest of the soldiers too. We've killed each of them mercilessly," said Aditya.

"It was not a righteous way to win a battle. We've already lost it when Samhati disarmed me in that duel. And rest of all our actions were completely unjustifiable," clarified Mahendra.

Aditya was going to say something in reply, but the upcoming unfortunate events did not let him speak. A heavy wind, coming from somewhere began to blow around him. As soon as the wind blew, he saw his father was disappearing from there. He became transparent like glass. He was so transparent that Aditya was able to see through his body.

"What's happening, father?" shouted Aditya in fear.

The severed head of Vikarna was still lying there. Aditya looked at it, and saw in the dim light of twilight that the eyes of Vikarna's head were open, and those were staring at Aditya. Aditya was frightened, and he was stepping backward to maintain a safe distance from the head.

Suddenly Vikarna's head moved its lips, and began to speak, "You are going to lose everything."

Just after that, the head disappeared into thin air.

Aditya continued stepping backward, stumbling, and he saw his father had disappeared already, and all of the soldiers of Kuru were disappearing one by one, and all the dead bodies of Anga's soldiers were gone too.

In the end, Aditya realized that his surroundings were so clear that no one would say that they had fought a war a while ago. There was no trace of blood anywhere on the field. All the soldiers along with the chariots, horses, elephants, and weapons, everything vanished from there.

Aditya was standing alone on the deserted ground, and the last supernatural event happened.

His dress up like a prince changed suddenly. His armor was gone, and the sword which he carried disappeared too.

Disappointed by losing everything, greatly surprised by those incidents that had happened subsequently after the battle, helpless Aditya was standing on the barren land alone, thinking of what he should do now to escape from the miserable condition.

Chapter Three

The cart-puller

Aditya was weeping like a little boy, and he kept on weeping for hours sitting on a rock, nearby of the deserted land where Aditya remained as the sole witness of a battle of extreme bloodshed. What kind of sorcery could it be? The entire army of Kuru, and his father diffused in air, without leaving any trace of them - just after Vikarna wished such, and the magic had happened - Aditya was talking to himself. He felt a strong desire for retaliation, but the person, who was responsible for all these unfortunate events, was already dead. Alas, there was no possible technique to harm a dead person.

As the night was getting darker, Aditya felt cold. It diverted his mind a bit from the pain of losing everything, and he required a shelter where he could spend the night.

Now he thought, after his father, he was the person who would take the authority as an emperor of Kuru. He should start the journey towards Kuru, he decided. He got up from the rock, and searched for someone who would provide him food and shelter for tonight.

Aditya was travelling along the same path, through which Kuru's army had come in the morning to conquer Anga. Was there any locality nearby? Aditya tried to recall, but could not. He just continued moving forward.

He had travelled a long distance, yet there was no sign of any abode of Anga's citizens. Even he did not see anyone in that deserted land. Did Vikarna's sorcery abolish every single person from the earth except him? Aditya thought it, and soon changed the thought as it would be a very bad idea to imagine the world human less. It could not be.

Suddenly Aditya felt pain in his stomach as he was hungry. He was thirsty too. He halted for a moment and looked at the moon. It was not perfectly a full moon, but nearly of it, and its brightness was enough for him to search his meal. He was looking for any tree of edible fruits which could suppress his hunger and thirst for the night. Alas, he had left behind some of the trees of that kind while travelling. He should have considered them before; he regretted.

A while later, Aditya managed to find an apple tree on the roadside, and it was covered with ripe apples. He plucked some of those, and fed himself as much as he was able to.

After the meal, he felt tired. An unwanted drowsiness did not let him continue the search for a shelter anymore, and he fell asleep under that tree as soon as he closed his eyes.

*****

Aditya woke up next morning when sunrays fell on his closed eyes. Just after waking up, he needed a while to realize what the hell had happened to him, recalling the entire incident that had happened yesterday. It was not easy to accept for a prince like Aditya finding himself, lying under an apple tree on a certain morning. He did not feel the softness of his bed that he used to feel every morning, he did not get the fragrance of his room that pervaded all time, he did not see the familiar walls of his room, and above all he did not feel the security as a prince. Tears broke out from his eyes, but he restrained from weeping, as he realized that merely weeping could not be a way of getting out of the trouble.

He continued the journey towards Kuru. First of all, he needed a vehicle or a horse to travel, as the route from that deserted place to the castle was long. He had not met anyone yet who would help him to reach his destination. He kept on walking as he did not have any other choice.

When the sun reached its zenith, he met someone who could help him finally. Aditya saw that a cart was coming from the distance, and it was pulled by a pair of bullocks, and driven by a village man of around thirty years of age.

Aditya stopped him, waving his hand, and said, "Take me to Kuru. Prepare your cart very fast. I'm in a hurry."

"Pardon me Sir, I'm also in a hurry, and I've lots of work to do today. Furthermore, Kuru is a long distance away from here, which would take several days to reach. It'll be not possible for me to take you there," said the cart-man in a polite tone.

It was the first time for him that he received a straight denial from someone apart from his father. He believed that his father had had the sole authority to refuse his demand. If someone refused to fulfil his demand, he considered it as a crime, and gave him a punishment later.

This time Aditya felt the same at first, but then he thought that the cart-man did not know his true identity. If he knew that, he would not dare to refuse.

Aditya considered that he should keep his true identity secret until he arrived at the castle. A disguise would be a good idea to keep himself away from any danger. Rather showing him greed for money seemed to be a good idea, decided Aditya.

"Listen, I am a very rich person, and I can give you enough money. That amount of money you can never imagine," said Aditya.

"Still I can't. If you offered me your entire property, I couldn't. My boss is waiting for me, and if I don't go there, he'll expel me from my day job."

Aditya became dejected for a moment, then he tried again bringing a clever smile on his face, "I would give you so much money, that you preferred to leave your day job forever. Not only that, at least your seven heirs would not require to do any day job. Just think of it."

The cart-man began to think, and he kept on thinking. After a long pause he answered, "Alright, I agree to take you there. But.."

A smile of instant relief appeared on Aditya's face, but it disappeared again when he listened to 'but'.

"But?" frowned Aditya.

"But, before we start the journey, I've to meet my boss once to let him know that I'll be absent at my workplace for several days."

"It's not necessary as you're going to leave your job soon."

"No, it's still necessary. He is waiting for me there. He knows I must come today, and he'll keep on waiting. If I go with you without informing him, or giving him a good reason for my absence, certainly a bad reputation will arise in his mind about my character that I am not sincere about my job. When the absence will be repeated for several days, he will consider me as not a trustworthy person at all. That way, I might become a person of inferior quality who could never be trusted," clarified the cart-man.

"If you get a chance to escape from me, you'll not return, I know," said Aditya in a tone of disbelief.

It seemed that the cart-man did not like the tone. He delivered a strong reply.

"Just think what kind of irony it is. You are not ready to trust me for once, and you insist that I go somewhere without notifying my boss. Isn't it unfair?" said the cart-man in a rude voice.

"Don't forget I can pay you so much money that neither you nor your boss have ever seen."

Aditya reminded the person about the money once more intending to boost up the craving for money, as he did not find any suitable reply of his logical words.

"If you offer the entire world to me, still I'm bound to meet my boss before the journey starts," said the cart-man, and he moved forward the vehicle towards his workplace.

"Then I'll give that money to another cart-man who will take me to the destination without arguing," warned Aditya.

"If you can, you do. Remember, you are not going to find anyone except me before travelling one hundred miles. Wait here, I must return within two hours," assured the cart-man while moving his cart.

Aditya saw that the cart-man moved away, without giving him a chance to negotiate.

Would he return, or did he just go off forever, and never would return? The cart-man had said, Aditya would not be able to meet anyone until he would walk a hundred miles more?

Did he tell the truth, or did he want to hang him back so that Aditya would remain as his customer, and the cart-man would become the sole recipient of the money that Aditya had promised?

Nevertheless, if he really wanted the money, why did he leave? Of course a hungry lion would never let go of its prey. The poor cart-man should behave like a hungry lion, and he should not let go his valuable customer away at any cost. What kind of force had driven him to relinquish greed?

Several questions, and thoughts were coming and going in Aditya's mind, and he was thinking what he should do next. Should he move forward, and look for another vehicle, considering the statement of the cart-man as a lie, or wait for him considering the statement was truth.

He kept on thinking, yet was hesitating to take any decision. Almost half an hour passed, then a curiosity came into his head. If he left the place that moment, he would never know whether the cart-man had returned or not. An unresolved mystery would haunt him in the future. And a feeling of repentance would act on him that he might have waited a few hours to check the truthfulness of the cart-man.

On the other hand, if he would wait here for a few hours, he would be able to get the answer that he was looking for. Not only that, If he would return, Aditya would get a company in that barren land. And if the worst case would happen that he did not return, Aditya would find out the man later, and punish him for his crime. There was no restriction to punish Anga's citizens now, as after the war, Anga became his territory.

At last, Aditya decided to wait there for a few hours more for the return of that cart-man.

Aditya sat on a nearby rock, and waited for the cart-man. Time to time, he was looking at the sun to estimate how much time he had spent waiting for him. As time passed, Aditya feared that the cart-man was certainly not coming, and he had wasted the entire time doing nothing. The sun inclined at the west, and that way it would set like everyday. He waited a long period for him, and he deserved a strong punishment, Aditya determined.

He stood up, and continued the search for another vehicle.

He just moved a few steps away from the initial position where he had met the cart-man, and at that moment he heard a voice from behind, "Wait! Where are you going? I've come."

Aditya turned around, and found the cart-man returned, as he had promised.

"Why did you delay?" asked Aditya, showing him anger.

"I'm not late at all, instead I came here early. Look at the sun. It's only been one and a half hours since I left," argued the cart-man.

"I presumed that you were not coming at all. However, the greed of money fetched you here," said Aditya.

"Your idea is incorrect," said the man, "It was not for the money, but the value of my words. I had to return not greed for money, but I promised you so."

"No one cares to keep promises nowadays," remarked Aditya.

"I do, and it comes from my inside. That's why when you insisted that I take you to Kuru, I had to meet my boss first to tell him, I would be unable to be present at my workplace for several days. It did not matter how much money you would pay; I would remain stubborn at my words."

"But, you didn't promise anything to your boss. It was only me, wasn't it?"

"No, things don't work like that. When I joined an employee under the supervision of my boss, I made an unspoken agreement that I would be obliged to be present everyday at my workplace. If any unavoidable circumstance doesn't allow me to be present for a day or days, I should tell the justifiable reason to my boss. I am bound to do this, every time," said the cart-man.

Aditya did not speak any. He was just thinking what he would do if he were the cart-man, in place of that person. Would he ever be able to resist himself from the hunger of money if someone offered him? Of course not. He would agree for the journey instantly without thinking twice, and never wanted to meet his employer again.

"Sire."

Aditya's attention broke as the cart-man called him.

"Yes," responded Aditya.

"Kuru is an enormous kingdom. Which place of Kuru do you wish to go to?" asked the cart-man.

"Hastinapur, the capital of kuru, take me there," replied Aditya.

Chapter Four

Everything had changed

"How dare you insult me that way?" broke out Aditya in anger while talking with a soldier of Kuru.

"I've just asked your identity," said the soldier in amazement.

"What kind of fun is going on here? Didn't you recognize me? Don't you know I am Aditya, the honorable prince of Kuru?"

The soldier stared at him as if he saw a ghost before him. Aditya could not understand why the soldier considered him as a stranger. All the soldiers should be aware that he was being a king.

The soldier spoke after a long pause, "Don't go anywhere. I'm coming within a few moments."

The soldier left without giving Aditya a chance to argue further.

After a seven days long journey, Aditya finally arrived at Kuru, and when the cart reached near his own castle, a soldier suddenly obstructed him from entering his abode, refusing to recognize him as the prince. The cart-man was still there, standing along with his cart a few feet away from the spot where the quarrel between Aditya and the soldier was going on. He was unable to hear the topic of the conversation from that distance.

But the cart-man predicted something serious would be going to happen.

He came closer to Aditya, and said, "Give me that money what you promised. I have to travel a long distance again to reach my home."

"Wait for a while until the soldier comes. Probably he's gone to fetch others to serve me a better welcome."

"I could not understand, why would they welcome you?" asked the surprised cart-man.

Aditya smiled, "I haven't revealed my true identity yet because of my personal security during the journey. Now the journey is over, and I've arrived at my destination, so it's the perfect moment to reveal my identity to you. I am Aditya, the son of the greatest emperor Mahendra. I am the only scion of the Kuru dynasty. Aren't you happy realizing that the prince of Kuru was with you all over the journey?"

At that moment it seemed that someone had taken away all the happiness from the cart-man's face. It became pale and dark. He shouted like an angry beast, "Are you insane? Don't you know that the queen had given birth to a dead son, and till today the king Mahendra is childless. Perhaps I could have realized earlier that I've been with a crazy man..."

The cart-man could not finish the sentence as they heard the shouting of soldiers from behind.

"Seize both of them," shouted one of them.

Aditya could not resist the soldiers because they had tied his hands before he could realize what was going on here. After that, the soldiers put them into separate prison cells.

*****

Next morning, they were presented at the royal court, and what Aditya experienced was entirely incredible for him.

The emperor was sitting on the throne as usual, and it was none other than Mahendra, Aditya's father, who had disappeared before his eyes. There was more surprise for him when he looked at the royal seat next to the emperor's throne. A beautiful lady was sitting on it. Aditya could recognize her. He had seen a painting of her hanging from the wall adjacent to his father's bedroom. He knew that the painting was of his mother, and she had died when Aditya was a baby. Now he saw the impossible. His mother was not a dead person anymore, but very alive. She was frequently chatting with her husband, and smiling. She was looking gorgeous, far more beautiful and gorgeous than the portrait of her.

How nice it would be if she could see Aditya here, and call him closer to adore. Aditya could not resist himself to seek her attention, breaking the basic etiquette of a court.

"Matasree (mother), you're alive! Pitasree (father), you are too!" called out Aditya as loud as he could.

It sought everyone's attention at him in the royal court. Whoever were present there looked at Aditya as they were seeing a crazy person in the middle of the courtroom. It seemed a few of them began to consider Aditya's claim as a truth. They whispered to each other indistinctly.

A royal person stood up from his chair, and ordered, "Silence!"

Then there persisted a pin drop silence around the royal court.

Aditya broke the silence again, "Father, I'm Aditya, your son, can't you recognize me?"

A soldier standing behind beat him hard as soon as Aditya shouted out again.

"You never told me that you are a father of a son. Who is his mother? Reveal to me," scolded Aditya's mother, widening her eyes.

"No dear, I see him for the first time."

Then he frowned at Aditya, "How dare you call me father? I never had a son. Nevertheless, according to the rule of my kingdom, you are given a chance to prove yourself. Tell me what proof you have from your side."

His own father, whom he knew since his childhood, now refused to recognize him as his son. Aditya realized everything. He realized how the curse had changed the entire scenario around him. He was now living in a new kind of world where he was not a prince anymore. Everything that had belonged to him once, was taken away.

Still he dictated everything from the beginning to convince the king.

Mahendra listened to the entire story, and finally Mahendra concluded, "What you have said is entirely rubbish. No doubt you're certainly suffering from an incurable mental illness, and it may cause damage to others. Kuru's prison was not made for crazy people, and Kuru is not a suitable place for them. On the other hand, no punishment is allowed to be given to any insane here according to the rule of Kuru, but they have to leave my territory forever. Soon my soldiers will take you out of Kuru."

Then Mahendra asked the audience, "Do you agree with my judgement?"

"Yes Maharaj (my king)," agreed everyone.

Mahendra turned around the cart-man, and asked the soldiers, "What's his crime?"

"Maharaj, he assisted the man to enter Kuru," replied a soldier.

"Maharaj, I am an ordinary cart-man, and poor too. He insisted that I should take him here. He promised me that he would pay a large amount of money."

"How much money has he promised to pay?" asked Mahendra.

"He did not tell me the amount, but he promised me that he would pay me so much that the money would not end even after my seventh generation," said the cart-man.

"Did you promise the same?" asked Mahendra.

"Yes," replied Aditya.

"Do you have that money?" asked Mahendra again.

"No, I don't. I've lost everything," said Aditya in pain, and tear drops came out from his eyes.

Mahendra said to the cart-man, "I am not finding any crime of yours, instead you are a sufferer of his insanity. That crazy boy was unable to pay you, yet you did your service well. Since you are a poor man, you deserve that money, I am willing to pay you the same amount from my treasury. After receiving the money, you are free to go anywhere."

The cart-man's face shone with happiness as soon as he heard the judgement from Mahendra.

Mahendra asked again to the audience, "Are you happy with my judgement?"

"Yes Maharaj," answered the applauding audience.

Aditya gazed at his father and mother thinking how happy they would have been, if he were not born. Everything seemed normal in their lives without having Aditya. They did not feel any deficiency of Aditya at all.

A soldier pushed on his back insisting him to move forward. Aditya turned his eyes at the floor, and closed them. A few drops of tears touched the floor coming out from his eyes. He looked at those drops of tears, and sighed. But he was compelled to move forward as the soldier pushed him again from behind.

Chapter Five

Nowhere to go

A lonely teenage boy, who had just crossed his eighteen, was wandering pointlessly through a long road. Having no idea where the road was leading him. Maybe it had a sudden dead end near a ridge, or it would lead him to a seashore. Maybe it would become narrower, and lead him into a deep forest where wild animals would end his life tearing his body with their sharp claws and teeth. Or it might end in a desert where he would cry out for water, but no sound would come out due to the dryness of his throat, and that way the tremendous thirst would be the cause of his death.

Was the road leading him to death? He asked himself, and simultaneously a fear of death ran through his spine. He halted for a moment, and turned around. Then he realized again that no return would be possible. Kuru's soldiers had gone away a long ago after giving him a warning not to return Kuru again.

Kuru, the enormous land where he had spent eighteen years since his childhood, now became a forbidden land for him. Not only that, the boy who used to be the prince of that kingdom, now became an ordinary person with no recognition.

There had been dozens of dedicated servants who were always engaged for him, and used to do their job according to his need. Thousands of soldiers who belonged to Kuru were ready to die for him. Every citizen of Kuru bowed down before him showing him respect.

His father, the emperor of Kuru loved him so much that he did not start his day before meeting him.

Now the situation did not remain the same. His existence had been erased from everyone's head, and they would consider him insane whenever he would try to convince them about the reality. His existence became an absurd phenomenon.

What would be his identity then? Aditya, the former prince of Kuru? No, he was not a prince, he had never been a prince according to the perception of others.

A boy with no identity, a boy having no destination to go, a boy having no home to stay, a boy having no money to spend, kept on walking like a vagabond.

What would be the next? Was he going to die that way? He was not feeling hungry or thirsty anymore. All his appetite had gone away after getting the shock, and he had no ability to think anymore about anything.

After travelling a long distance from Kuru, the boy fell down on the empty road losing his consciousness.

*****

"Aditya, Aditya."

Aditya was getting back his sense as he heard a male voice that was calling him by his name. He slowly opened his eyes, but could not see anyone in the moonlit night.

"Aditya, Aditya."

He could hear his name again. He tried to estimate the direction from which the voice was coming. It was coming from the direction of an enormous fig tree which stood at the roadside.

Aditya looked there, and found a shadowy human figure standing under the tree.

If he existed in a different kind of world now, how could it be possible for someone to know his name? Aditya asked himself.

"Who is speaking there? Reveal yourself. Let me see your face," demanded Aditya.

Yet the figure did not move from its place.

"How is everything going on Aditya?" asked the figure.

Aditya stood up, and slowly stepped towards the human figure.

He shouted again, "Didn't you listen to me? Come out from the shadows."

The figure moved forward a few steps, and halted.

His face was revealed in the moonlight. Aditya recognized him.

"Impossible! I've killed you by my own hand," exclaimed Aditya.

It was Vikarna. Aditya had severed his head on the battlefield, and witnessed his death before his eyes. It was extremely impossible to see him alive.

Aditya rushed towards him like an insane, and said, "I am not going to spare you now. You have taken away everything from me. Release me from the curse, and return everything that I had."

Aditya tried to punch on his face, but he missed, as his fist could not get him, and went through air.

"How can you harm a person who is already dead, Aditya?" said Vikarna.

"If you are dead, how are you speaking to me?"

"It is merely my soul," said Vikarna.

"How can I talk to a soul? Am I also dead?" asked Aditya.

"Almost," replied Vikarna.

"Oh!"

"You are lying at the junction of life and death. What have you decided, Aditya? Do you want to die?" asked Vikarna.

"No, I want to live. I have to live. I want to get my previous life back. Take back your curse. Take back your damn curse now," demanded Aditya angrily.

"It is as impossible as you are unable to make me alive again."

"Then there will be no reason to live. Staying alive will be a burden for me. How can I stay alive, renouncing all those happiness and facilities that I enjoyed as a prince?"

"So, you have decided to die? Remember, you are at the junction of life and death, and your decision will lead you to the desired state. Now answer me. What have you chosen between the two? Live or death?"

Aditya kept on thinking for a long moment, then he finally answered.

"I want to live."

"It's good to see that you have chosen wisely. You shall live."

After a pause, Vikarna added, "Travelling seven miles more, you will find a village where you can get required food and shelter."

"How can I get there? I became so weak from starving for several days that I barely could walk a few steps more. Seven miles is an unimaginably long distance for me."

"You have to," said Vikarna's soul, "Tomorrow morning you will feel better as you chose to live. You can definitely go there."

"And how can I avail food and shelter there?"

"Begging might be the best idea," replied Vikarna.

"Never! A prince cannot beg door to door," said Aditya aggressively.

"It seems you'll never be successful in abolishing the curse," smiled Vikarna.

"What did you say? Is there any way to eliminate it?" asked Aditya.

"Yes, there is a way."

"Tell it to me," demanded Aditya.

"Let it go. You'll never be able to achieve it. It's a very difficult task for you."

"Please tell me about the way. I can do anything to get my past life back."

"Alright, I am revealing the way. Listen to me carefully. The curse can be broken when you will feel from your heart that your present life is much better than the past one."

"Are you joking to me? I'll never be going to love this cursed life. Tell me another way to remove the curse."

"Ha... Ha... Ha...," laughed Vikarna's soul.

"There is only one way to remove the curse," echoed Vikarna's voice, and he disappeared from there.

Aditya felt sick again after the disappearance of Vikarna, and fell on the ground losing consciousness.

Chapter Six

Hesitance

Was it a dream? Definitely it was not.

Aditya was stunned as he regained consciousness in the morning. He found himself lying under the fig tree. Veer recalled when he had lost consciousness yesterday, he had fallen down in the middle of the road. First he could not understand how he got there. Then he recalled the conversation between him and Vikarna's soul, which was seemingly a dream to Aditya.

But, now he realized the incident must have been the truth, otherwise the abnormal shift of his lying position was impossible to explain.

He felt physically much better than yesterday for an unknown reason. Vikarna's soul had said that it would be so, thought Aditya.

At the next moment, he felt angry, recalling the entire meeting with Vikarna's soul. Probably he had not been in full consciousness. If he had been, he could not have dealt with him in such a polite manner. Aditya regretted thinking of his own deficiency.

Then he recalled the moment when Vikarna's soul had revealed the way to break the curse. It would be better if he did not tell him the way, because there could be no reason to love this life forgetting the past life as a prince, Aditya thought.

What would be the future then? If the curse would remain intact, would he be going to live as an ordinary person for the rest of his life?

Impossible! He was not going to stay as an ordinary man forever.

But there was no other way out.

Aditya gave up thinking much. No one could tell how much he was going to suffer in the near future.

Suddenly he felt hungry. Since the moment of exile from Kuru, he had forgotten to eat or drink. Again he felt the need for food and water.

Aditya began the journey again. After travelling two to three miles, he found a pond, and yielded a long breath of relaxation looking at it. Finally, he was going to drink some water.

He removed his clothes, and kept them on the bank, and jumped into the pond. The water was so clear that he was able to see its floor. He drank lots of water pouring into his stomach, but it was unable to reduce his hunger at all.

After taking the bath, Aditya continued walking in search of food and shelter. If there really existed a village as Vikarna has mentioned, he would get there within a few hours.

Had Vikarna's soul said the truth? Would it be a good idea to trust him? After all, Vikarna was his enemy, and Aditya was murderer of him. He might want to end

Aditya's life too, due to an indomitable desire for vengeance. Maybe Aditya could die if he went there.

What would Aditya do if someone ruined his life? Aditya asked himself. Soon he corrected himself as he realized his life was already ruined. However, he was still alive, and his existence might be the only thing remaining that he could claim as his property. Did Vikarna's ghost want to take away his life too? If Aditya were in Vikarna's condition, he would definitely want the same.

Aditya halted, and looked behind along the road that had been travelled by him. If he took about-turn, he would arrive again at Kuru. But Kuru did not remain a safe place for him. If Kuru's soldiers found him there, they would kill him without showing any mercy. If he would stop walking, and stay here, he would die too because of starvation. There was no other option but moving forward.

Then he recalled the past incident when he had waited for the cart puller's return. At the end, he returned as he had promised. He had proven himself as a truthful person. What would he lose if he considered Vikarna's soul had spoken the truth?

After a lot of thinking, Aditya finally made a decision to move forward. No other provision was available for him. He found all of these would lead him to death.

Chapter Seven

Kali, the demon

Indeed, there existed a village, as Aditya could see it from a distance, after travelling the exact path that had been mentioned by Vikarna. Aditya looked around, and observed a magnificent view. He never imagined such a place like heaven could exist on earth. So many beautiful places belonged to Kuru, but none of those could be compared to the beauty of that place, Aditya thought.

There was an enormous waterfall situated in the distant mountain. Water was continuously flowing down from it into a large lake, and the lake was decorated with several water flowers. Most of them were lotus flower of different colors, and other kinds were unknown to Aditya.

A narrow river, which originated from the lake, flowed through the village. Aditya tried to survey the village from there, and he discovered that it was an abode of poor people who were not seemingly able to run their lives in luxury. Probably they were so poor that they could barely manage their food everyday. Aditya predicted so after carefully noticing the condition of their houses. Those were either made of mud or wood, but a few of them were made of polished rocks. It was not hard to conclude that owners of the rock made houses were wealthier than others. However, they were not wealthy enough to provide Aditya a generous hospitality. Despite the beauty of that place, he was unable to stay there for a long period, thought Aditya.

Right at the moment, he just needed food and shelter to survive. He decided to enter the village expelling other thoughts from his mind.

"Do you really want to go there?"

Who could be talking to him in the deserted land? Aditya was surprised for a moment. He turned around, and found no one there. Maybe it was a hallucination created by starvation for a long period, thought Aditya.

He continued walking.

"Please, don't go there."

Aditya heard the voice again, and he turned around to see the person. This time he found a person standing there.

"Who are you? There was no one a few moments ago. But now I see you appeared from nowhere. Where do you come from?" asked Aditya.

Aditya observed his appearance. The man looked very ugly. He was uglier than the ugliest man in the world could ever be possible. Aditya could not tolerate the ugliness of his face. He moved his eyes to another direction to get rid of seeing him.

The ugly man answered, "I am Kali. I live inside you."

"Do not try to trick me. What do you think I'm a child, or a mindless stupid who will believe anything that you say?" said Aditya angrily.

"I'm speaking the truth, dear Aditya. I live inside you from the beginning. Staying within you, I have been watching you from the first day of your life. I have directed to you the easiest way to remove every obstacle in life. Till today, you acted accordingly following my directions. In that battle, when your father was disarmed and felt helpless, I directed you to shoot an arrow to Samhati, and you performed well. I directed you to kill all the soldiers of your opponent, and you did exactly what I wanted. Even you beheaded your captive Vikarna because of me."

"Stop this nonsense! I did everything because I wished the same."

"Yes, you said right. You wished so. But I am the person who implemented the wish inside your mind. You are my favorite host, Aditya. Your every action makes me happier, and you nourish me so well that I become stronger and healthier within you."

Aditya was gradually believing his speech. In this world, no one would be aware about the battle, or about his real father except Aditya himself. Possibly the person was telling the truth. Still he had several doubts.

Aditya said, "No person is able to live inside another. Tell me who you are."

"I am not a human being. I am Kali, a demon. You are not the sole host of mine, rather everybody carries a small part of mine. Those who obey my instructions perfectly, my parts become stronger within them."

"And what happens to those who do not obey you?" asked Aditya curiously.

"Without proper nourishment, those parts become weak, and eventually I leave them forever."

"I understand," said Aditya, "But I wonder why you're resisting me to enter the village?"

"Because I fear that if you go there, you may refuse to obey me further. It will make me weak."

"You're just well concerned about your own profit. Probably you forget, I've been starving for several days. If I don't get food, my death will be certain," said Aditya, and he paused for a moment. Aditya spoke again, "Alright then, if you wish that I should not go there, I'll not go. But you have to arrange the necessary food and shelter for me right now."

"I'm sorry, I can't. I possess no ability to deliver physical things to my hosts. I can only provide stimulation in someone's mind, so that he can choose the easiest path to overcome a problem."

"Oh, then I have another demand which I need most. Tell me a way, following which I can get back my life as a prince again."

The demon did not answer any. He remained silent.

Aditya turned up his voice, "What happened? Tell me the way, which will return everything that I have lost."

"I haven't any," said Kali remorsefully.

"Then you are not useful to me. I have sufficient ability to make decisions of my own. I don't need you anymore. Stay away from me." said Aditya rudely.

"I can't stay away from you. You're my favorite host. If I leave you, my power will be diminished. How can I live without you?"

Aditya observed that the demon transformed itself into a dark shadow, and after that the shadow dissolved into Aditya's body.

*****

When Aditya finally arrived at the village, he felt exhausted. He spent his entire energy travelling there. He waited for the villagers expecting a warm welcome from them. Probably he had forgotten for the moment that he did not remain a prince anymore. He observed that all the villagers were busy in their respective professions.

A group of farmers were harvesting crops in the field. They did not even notice that an outsider entered the village. They remained engaged at their work without any break. Aditya decided to ask them the name of the place, but he could not as he was feeling weak.

He moved ahead through the lane, which led him to a locality where the huts were nicely arranged on both sides. Although the huts congested the place a little, the neatness of their arrangement enhanced the overall beauty. Each hut had been built maintaining a fixed distance with others, and their appearances were quite different from usual. He had never seen such a design in Kuru.

Huts were generally built in the shape of rectangular boxes, but Aditya noticed that here the huts were cylindrical, and their roofs were shaped like farmers' hats.

All those huts were full of greenery. Every owner decorated his hut with several trees and plants. Even their roofs were also covered with grasses. At the entrances of the huts, villagers had planted several trees that made the place well furnished.

Aditya noticed among the trees, there were a few trees containing fruits. Aditya was determined to pluck some fruits from the trees, staying hidden from the villagers.

There were a few villagers who were busy with their work near the entrance of the respective huts. Aditya observed a poor father with his two sons who were weaving baskets with twigs, and piling up them aside. When Aditya came to them, they just glanced at Aditya for once, and remained busy again. They did not show any activity to help Aditya, or asked him anything.

Aditya turned around another hut, where a middle aged woman was helping her husband in repairing the window of their hut. Her husband was a potter. Several clay pots were stored in the front of the hut, and a potter's wheel was also there. That family did not even notice Aditya's presence.

Aditya was finding a scope of stealing fruit from someone's tree. A while later, he finally found the desired circumstance in his surroundings. There was no one, and every door was shut around him. Probably they were sleeping, thought Aditya.

He found a banana tree full of ripe bananas. He looked around like a thief to confirm that no one was watching him. After being confirmed, he plucked some ripe bananas, and began to eat.

He had just finished half of a banana, and right at that moment, he felt a powerful thrust on his chest. The thrust came from an invisible origin, and it was so powerful that it lifted Aditya's body in the air, and he landed on the ground a few steps away from the previous position. His head hit something solid, and before he could realize what had happened to him, he lost consciousness due to severe pain.

Chapter Eight

A place like a prison

When his consciousness returned, Aditya found himself lying on a bed in a small room. He was trying to comprehend how he got here. Meanwhile a middle aged man, around fifty years old, entered the room opening the wooden door carrying a clay pot in his hand.

"Good to see you're awake," smiled the person. Then he handed over the pot to Aditya, and said, "Drink it. You'll feel better."

Aditya took the pot, and saw it contained milk. He asked, holding the pot carefully with both hands, "Where am I? How did I come here?"

"This place is called Dharmkhet, and you're at my home, boy. When I saw you lying on the road unconscious, I brought you here."

Aditya finished the milk at once, and recalled the incident that happened before he became unconscious.

"Yes, I remember. An invisible fist punched on my chest, and after that my head hit a rock, and I became unconscious," said Aditya.

That man smiled, "Definitely you did something wrong before that incident happened."

"What do you mean, I did wrong. I did nothing. I was just eating bananas from a tree," said Aditya.

"Did you asked for a permission from the owner of that tree, before taking off the bananas?"

"No, I didn't."

"Then you have obviously committed a sin. You were stealing someone's property. Are you a thief?"

"No, I am not a thief," shouted Aditya angrily, "I am......"

He was about to say that he was the prince of Kuru. But, soon he controlled himself realizing that his true identity had been taken away.

"I am Aditya, only Aditya," said Aditya mournfully.

"Listen Aditya, I don't know who you are, or where you came from. But, if you want to stay in this land, you have to follow a simple rule. The rule is that you should not do any sin."

"What will happen if I do anything what I want to do? Who is going to bother about my activities all the time?"

"Ha... Ha... Ha...," laughed the person, "Vikranta will bother. He is watching you all the time. He has been watching the activities of all the people in this land since many years. If you repeat the mistake again, stay prepared to suffer from his punishment again."

"Who is Vikranta? There was no one in front of me when I got the punch. Does Vikranta stay invisible?"

"He is a dead person, Aditya. He became a soul, and lives among us, no one knows from when. He had been here when my grandfather lived. Even my grandfather's grandfather also experienced him. Maybe he has been living here for a thousand years or more."

"You are sounding ridiculous. You meant to say that a ghost has punched me?"

"Exactly so," said the man patiently.

A few days ago he used to be a non-believer of ghosts, but after the battle, he experienced the presence of Vikarna's soul that made him believe in any supernatural entity.

He stayed silent for a moment, and after that, he began uttering, "I'm not going to stay here. I don't want to stay in a place where a ghost interferes with people's lives."

Aditya stood up from the bed intending to go outside.

"Everybody does the same for the first time," mumbled the man himself.

Then he said, "Listen to me, Aditya. You should try it tomorrow. But, it's already night time. If you go outside now, several dangers may happen to you. I'm going to prepare our dinner. I hope that you would prefer to sleep after the meal."

The person left the room delivering the short instruction.

*****

Aditya was served a very simple meal. It consisted, rice made of the cheapest grain available, a bowl soup of lentils, and a curry prepared with several vegetables. It was the first time after getting his new identity that he was going to taste something cooked apart from those fuites. Being a prince, he had never eaten any food of that kind that was cooked for ordinary people.

How disgusting the food was going to be. Still, if he wanted to survive, should have to eat the thing, he thought. But when the person brought the served plate closer to Aditya, he received a nice smell from it.

He took a small nibble from the plate, and poured it into his mouth. Surprisingly, he got a heavenly satisfaction at that moment. The taste was awesome. It was tastier than any food that he had ever eaten. He began to eat like a hungry monster.

The person was sitting by him. He noticed how Aditya was hurriedly consuming his food.

He said, "Your food is not going anywhere.

You may eat gently."

Aditya was a little embarrassed. Of course it was not good manners. He began to eat gently.

During the dinner, he came to know several things about the person. His name was Daruk. Several generations of him had lived in Dharmkhet. Once he had a family, his wife and daughter. But for a decade, he lived alone in his home. Aditya asked him what had happened to them. Daruk did not answer that question, but cried.

Aditya understood that Daruk was an emotional person. He should not have asked about his family. But he suspected there might be a mystery about his family.

*****

That night Aditya could not get asleep, and kept on waiting for the morning to come. At the moment when he saw a glimpse of light from the window, he slowly got up from the bed, and opened the door as quietly as possible.

Daruk was dead asleep in another room, he noticed. He stepped outside of the hut, and walked across the same road from which he had come to Dharmkhet. It seemed that the entire village was dead as there was no one outside in the early morning.

Aditya arrived at the spot from where the territory of Dharmkhet was started, and was about to leave the place. But another wonder was waiting for Aditya. Suddenly his entire body collided with something solid while he was moving fast to escape. He was stunned for a moment as he could not see any obstacle on his path. He tried again, but failed. Then he realized that an invisible obstacle was resisting him to move forward. It was nothing but a wall, but completely invisible to a person.

He tried to escape from another region, but the wall was also there. He kept on trying but the wall existed in every direction. He went east and west, south and north, but the wall did not let him to leave the village. He tried every possible method to overcome it. He tried to climb up on it, he tried to break it, even he tried to escape through the bottom of it digging the ground, but that endless impenetrable wall stood alone in his path. It ruined his intention of escaping the land by every possible manner.

Chapter Nine

Vikranta

A devastated Aditya reluctantly returned to Daruk's home. He saw Daruk was standing at the entrance of his hut. It seemed Daruk was waiting for his return. Aditya became angry when he observed a cute smile on Daruk's face.

Aditya burst out, "You knew that I would be unsuccessful to escape."

"Yes, I knew," replied Daruk patiently.

"Then why didn't you tell earlier about the wall?"

"I would tell you today if you met once before you left. But you did not give me the chance to tell," clarified Daruk.

After a pause, he continued, "What did you think, it would be very easy to leave the place? You were wrong. Do you know why this place is called Dharmkhet?"

"No," replied Aditya in an inaudible voice.

"This place is called Dharmkhet because Dharma is always protected here. Many people just like you had come here before, and encountered Vikranta's punishment. Even many of them were of evil personalities. Initially they'd all tried to escape from here, but they could not because of the existence of that indestructible wall. They had no other option but to stay here unwillingly. Eventually they didn't like Dharmkhet at first, but as time passed, they loved this place and stayed here."

"What do you mean, it is a place like a prison? Vikranta punishes them that way?"

"No, a prisoner stays in a prison unwillingly. But dwellers of Dharmkhet live here willingly. Vikranta taught them the true meaning of Dharma."

"I know the meaning of Dharma too. Dharma is nothing but some old fashioned customs and rituals written by our ancestors, and people should follow them blindly."

"You've mistaken. It's not the true meaning of Dharma at all. Those people who properly know the true meaning of Dharma, gain the capacity to differentiate good and evil, and eventually they choose the good one to lead their lives."

Aditya thought for a moment. He never judged anything in a good or a bad category. He always did what he wished to do. If he judged himself that way, he definitely appeared to be a sinful person.

He said, "I admire your way of thinking. But I couldn't understand why people are so obsessed about Vikranta. The ghost only knows how to punish people. He does not possess other qualities except that."

"Do not try to judge Vikranta's qualities. He is a good soul, and savior of these people. He is also protecting us from any severe harm. Even he saved many lives from the grasp of death. I believe that one day you'll also discover the greatness of Vikranta."

"If you believe that the ghost always does good things, why have your family members left you?" asked Aditya annoyingly.

Probably Daruk had no answer to that particular question. He remained silent.

Chapter Ten

Towards good, renouncing bad

Aditya had been staying as Daruk's guest for over one month. During those days, he had gathered knowledge about many rules and regulations, abiding by which, he was able to keep himself away from Vikranta's punishment. He learnt how to show respect to others, especially to elders. He learnt how to always speak the truth. He learnt how to become kind to people, renouncing selfishness. And, he learnt several other character building guidelines.

He was bound to maintain a good character merely to stay away from Vikranta. Whenever he wanted to do something unlawful, his subconscious mind always reminded him about the torturous punishment of Vikranta. Despite safeguards, he did many undesirable activities in those days, for which Vikranta had to punish him.

He was gradually becoming acquainted with the new place. He came to know that Dharmkhet did not belong to any king, though its territory was vast like a kingdom. Aditya wanted to know the history related to Dharmkhet, but the villagers could not help him as they knew nothing about the history.

In spite of the lack of a king, lifestyles of those villagers were going on well. Although they were poor, they were overflowing with happiness and peace. Aditya wondered sometimes how they could always stay happy. Were they acting, staying happy to impress Vikranta? But he might be wrong because he had never seen anyone who had had a complaint against the ghost - not even a single one.

Not every villager was always able to maintain a good character, and eventually they had to receive punishment from Vikranta for their wrong actions. Still they loved Vikranta unconditionally. How could it be possible?

Another strangeness compelled him to wonder. He always believed that a poor person was unable to find happiness as he did not possess enough money and wealth. But here he found the opposite. In spite of having an inadequate amount of wealth, they were far happier than Aditya when he used to be a prince.

He was unable to solve the mystery himself. One day he asked Daruk hesitatingly, "Can I ask a question to you?"

"Why are you hesitating? Please ask."

"I was thinking how these poor villagers are leading their lives happily, as I can see they are too poor to stay happy?"

Daruk smiled, "Who said that they are poor? And how are you so sure that wealth is a necessary thing to stay happy?"

"Yes, I know. Money and wealth are very necessary in our lives, as necessary as air that we breathe," said Aditya.

Daruk giggled, and said, "If those things have no value here, why should someone need it?"

"What do you mean to say? Money has no value?" asked Aditya curiously.

"We don't use any currency to buy things. Still we are able to get what we need," answered Daruk.

"How?"

"We work hard, and produce things. If we need something to buy, we simply go to those persons who produce that particular thing to sell. And we can buy that product by exchanging our product with them. For example, if you want to become the owner of a house, you have to buy required materials, and need a mason to build the house. You have to exchange something if you want to get those facilities."

Aditya thought for a moment, and said, "I understand. If people are spending their lives that way, why are some people relatively wealthier than others?"

"Several factors control the economy of these villagers. Everybody does his own work, but the efficiencies of individuals are different. They are able to earn accordingly."

"Please explain it to me elaborately," demanded Aditya.

"Their earnings are proportionately varying depending upon the quality and quality of their goods. Another factor is also responsible for the inequality to their economic conditions. Types of products that they produce, do not deserve equal values. Most of the people have usually chosen to work in the fields, which require limited skills, or no skill at all. Since they have chosen to perform easier works, their products or services are easily available in our village. As a result, the value of their works becomes cheaper. On the other hand, some services require special skills to perform. Definitely, their products or services deserve more value, and workers of those fields evidently have better lifestyles," clarified Daruk.

After a pause, he continued, "However, everyone finds happiness and peace in his own field, irrespective of their lifestyles. No one has any complaint or dissatisfaction about his earnings. And there is another group of people who have learnt to renounce their all desires. They have finally found the origin of all unhappiness in humans' lives, and they have abolished that origin through controlling their minds. They are able to stay calm in every situation in life, and prefer to lead their lives with very minimal requirements, which would solve the purpose of staying alive."

"They don't need to do much work then," remarked Aditya.

"They also do their jobs as well. But they don't work with an expectation to earn something from it. They do their jobs selflessly in order to improve society. They know the ultimate truth of life that everything is a lie."

"I couldn't understand. What is the lie?" asked Aditya curiously.

"Everything that belongs to us, is a lie. Everybody will die one day, and he will not be allowed to keep his wealth after his death."

Aditya was stunned listening to his words. What Daruk was saying was quite sensible. No human is allowed to carry his wealth after his death. He had never thought like that.

Daruk continued, "But there are a few things which stay along with a soul after death."

"What are those things? Let me know, please.," asked Aditya excitedly.

"Someone's virtues that he had earned when he lived. People would continue to talk about his goodness, good character, selflessness, and several other good things of that person for many days, and that way his soul achieves liberation peacefully."

"I am not a desireless person. I always owned the thing that I wanted most. But now I lost everything. I want to get back all those things that I lost," uttered Aditya.

"If you want anything in Dharmkhet, you have to earn the same. And you'll be able to earn a thing, when you'll spend something for it. Soon you have to leave my home, and start a job to become a self-reliant person," said Daruk.

Aditya did not expect that he was going to listen to a hard talk from him. He was shocked.

"I thought people are selfless here, and they take care of others. But you are going to expel your guest from your home? What kind of Dharma is it?" said Aditya, annoyed.

"You misunderstood me. There are many minor aspects of Dharma, which should have to be maintained. You are not a burden for me at all, but if I treat you as my guest for a long period, your nature will change permanently. That way you will always try to find a scope to live your life like a parasite, and according to the laws of Dharma, it is not deserved. One day you would find that your life became worthless, and then you would blame me that I did not let you learn how to become a self-reliant person. That is why I want to maintain my Dharma. Moreover, Vikranta will take steps against both of us if you continue to stay in my house for many days."

"I can understand now," said Aditya, "But I don't have any skill to do any work. How can I do a job? And please tell me, where will I live if you don't let me stay in your house?"

"Don't worry. I'll take you tomorrow to my friend. He will supervise you, and also teach you required skills to start your own work. And of course, you can stay at my home until you will make your own. But you have to pay me the rent for your staying," declared Daruk.

Chapter Eleven

Kaivartya

On the next morning, as per the direction of Daruk, Aditya was getting ready for the outing. He was quite reluctant to do any job willingly. But Daruk would not listen to him, if he refused. If Daruk did not provide shelter to Aditya in his home, he would have been suffering till today.

He finished all the necessary routine work in the early morning, and needed a good dress to look handsome near an unknown person. Although he owned only one dress from the beginning, he had borrowed a few more from Daruk, but those were not suitable for the purpose, thought Aditya.

He asked Daruk, "Do you have a good dress which I can use for today?"

Daruk was in another room adjacent to Aditya's room getting dressed. He answered from there, "See inside the wardrobe."

There was a wardrobe kept inside the room where Aditya was staying. He never opened it. Now he opened it for the first time, and took out a good looking robe from it. At the moment Aditya noticed there were several womens' dresses too. Aditya presumed those had been for Daruk's wife and daughter who were most probably dead now. Daruk did not reveal yet how they had died.

Along with those ladies' dresses, he found several ornaments made either of wood and clay. Aditya pondered how poor Daruk could be. He was so poor that even his wife was unable to own any gold or silver jewelry. Aditya closed the wardrobe, and put on the robe.

Daruk was already ready to go out, and he was waiting for Aditya in his room. When he saw Aditya was ready too, he left the hut along with Aditya closing the main entrance. There was no need for any lock, as no stealing or robbery was possible because Vikranta was looking after everyone's security all the time.

Aditya was thinking how he would be able to perform a job of ordinary people as once he used to be a prince. Daruk did not know the reality about Aditya. No one in Dharmkhet knew about his past. If he disclosed the truth to them, they would have considered him as insane like his own father had done.

In spite of that, Aditya was curious about the profession which Daruk decided for him. He asked, "Where are we going, and what is the profession I am going to choose?"

"Keep your patience, Aditya. Soon you will come to know."

"Still I am a little worried. What will happen if the profession does not suit me?"

"Don't worry. It suits all, and a very limited amount of skill is required to perform it. I'm going to tell you, but before that answer me a question," said Daruk.

"Please ask," said Aditya.

"Can you guess which profession earns maximum respect among all in Dharmkhet?" asked Daruk.

Aditya kept on thinking about the answer longer than usual. Aditya knew that a king or an emperor receives the highest honor in society, and then comes, minister, general, and other officials. But Dharmkhet had no king, therefore any of those positions did not exist.

"Did you guess?"

"Soldiers?" answered Aditya in a hurry, yet he knew that the answer was going to be wrong.

Daruk smiled, "Did you forget, soldiers have no work here? Vikranta is the sole protector of Dharmkhet, and he does not need any soldier. I'm giving you another chance."

"I couldn't guess," Aditya gave up.

"A teacher," answered Daruk, "Profession of teaching is considered to be superior among all others."

"Why?"

"Because a teacher plays a major role in our society. He builds the character of his students, those students make the future of society. It leads our civilization towards betterment. This is the only process of how our civilization evolves. A teacher should not sell his knowledge, but should spread it among people selflessly. A good teacher is able to make a huge progress, but a society of lack of teachers definitely would destroy."

"Am I going to be a teacher?" asked Aditya.

"No," said Daruk, "Huge amount of knowledge and skills are necessary to become a teacher. At your age, you do not possess the same. You have to gain it over time through your experience, if you want to be. If you deserve that position in society, people will make you a teacher automatically."

"Then what am I going to choose?"

"You are going to choose another respectful profession, which stands in second place."

"What is it?"

"Farming."

"Farming!"

Aditya was shocked. He disagreed, "As I knew, farmers are the poorest among all?"

"Who said that? Farmers' earnings are quite good. Even they earn more than teachers."

"Why is it so? You've already said that the teaching profession is most prestigious."

"Yes, it is true, but it is extremely unethical being a teacher to demand something from his students. Still, students are bound to give something to their master according to their capacities. But many students belong to poor families, and eventually they are unable to give much. On the other hand, a farmer produces food, which is the most necessary item for the people of all classes. Eventually, his earnings should be much higher. Probably you've noticed most of the families in Dharmkhet are farming something in their own houses, thus you can imagine how much precious food is."

Aditya was unable to deny his reasoning. He was aware about the necessity of food for survival. Once his life was about to end due to the lack of food.

Daruk brought him near the river, which originated from the lake. Aditya had seen the river once when he had come to the Dharmkhet for the first time.

"Are we going to cross it?" asked Aditya.

"No, we just arrived at our destination," said Daruk.

Standing at the riverbank, Aditya looked around, and found himself surrounded by an enormous agricultural land full of various crops.

A group of farmers were working in the field. They were preparing the land for sowing with the help of a pair of bullocks, which were tied to a wooden plough, and the farmers were holding the plough tightly to keep it steady. An enormous hut, looking like a warehouse, was situated at one side of the land. It was made of mud and wood, and its roof was covered with straws.

Daruk shouted at the farmers, pointing at the hut, "Is Kaivartya inside?"

They delivered a welcome smile to Daruk, and gave him affirmation of Kaivartya's presence nodding their heads. Aditya just came to know that he was going to work under someone's supervision, whose name was Kaivartya. Daruk went inside the hut, instructing Aditya to wait outside for a few moments.

A while later Daruk came out from the hut along with a person of the same age as Daruk. No doubt, the unknown person was Kaivartya.

His appearance was like a sage. His hair and beard was longer than usual, and he was covered with saffron cloth. A mysterious serenity persisted on his face, yet his body was quite muscular like a warrior. Moreover, he lived in a place where an unnatural tranquility always existed, as there was no other hut nearby of his abode.

After some trivial discussion he commanded Aditya to visit this place everyday from tomorrow onwards.

Chapter Twelve

Work is better than no work

Next day morning Aditya attended there. He was expecting Kaivartya would give him some tasks related to farming, but astonishingly Kaivartya just said to watch other farmers' activities, how they were cultivating crops in the field.

There could be no task easier than that. It was just to watch other people working, sitting somewhere. Aditya selected a wooden platform nearby the hut, and sitting on it, he could observe those farmers.

He spent the entire daytime sitting on the platform, watching the farmers. He observed how seeds were sowed in the field, how they applied fertilisers to the soil for the faster growth of plants, how to apply water to germinate the newly sowed seeds, and many trivial activities of the farmers. He also noticed Kaivartya went somewhere carrying a bunch of firewood when the sun was in the midst of the sky. When the sun was about to set, the farmers stopped their work, and were ready to go home.

Aditya could not decide what he should do now. Kaivartya had gone somewhere telling him not to go anywhere until he would return. When he was just going to lose his patience, Kaivartya returned. The bunch of firewood that he had carried, was not with him. Maybe he sold the firewood, or gave it to someone else. Kaivartya told him to wait a few more moments, and went inside his hut.

Then he came out carrying a bag full of something. Aditya noticed it contained food grains.

"It is your salary for today's work."

Aditya wondered a little. He did nothing today, but sat there all the time watching the activities of farmers. Why was Kaivartya offering him remuneration? That question arose in his mind, but he did not express it to him. He gladly accepted the remuneration, and came back to Daruk's home.

It was quite unexplainable how Aditya was feeling. The pain of losing everything was always acting on him, yet he was feeling good today. It was his first income in life. The bag full of grains was the only thing which he could claim as his own.

*****

On the next day, the same story repeated. He went to his workplace, and sat there throughout the day, and at the end, returned home with a bag full of grains.

Aditya knew well that the bags of grains had very little value to him. When he had been a prince, he owned many objects which were many times worthier than the grains. Still he was feeling happy being the owner of those bags for an unknown reason.

Moreover, he was surprised by Kaivartya's action. He was paying him without any reason. It was a matter of fun near Aditya. He wanted to taste that fun again and again, and indeed he did the same activity upto six days.

On the seventh day, Aditya began to feel bored. It seemed that doing no work was quite painful for him. Why was he feeling so? He asked himself. Any kind of work was always quite painful for him, but now he was feeling pain having no work!

Whatever the reason might be, he wanted to do something. Those working farmers were creating a mysterious sensation that he should join them, and help them in their work.

As he wished, he did so. A few farmers were sowing seeds on the ground. Aditya went to them, and took a portion of seeds, and sowed the seeds following the process of other farmers.

During the next few days, he preferred to help the farmers, instead of doing nothing. That way he learnt the basic techniques of cultivation of crops within a few days.

One day he expressed his wish near Kaivartya, "Please give me some work to do. I want to do something myself."

Kaivartya smiled. It seemed he wanted to hear those words from Aditya. He gave him a bag of barley seeds, and provided a piece of land for him, just telling, "Plant these seeds in this land, and show me your abilities."

Of course he was not going to fight a battle where he would have to show his ability. It was called farming, and it was as easy as it sounded. First of all, he would prepare the soil by digging the ground, and then he would have to sprinkle the seeds on the soil, and after that he would apply some water to germinate the seeds. And the next task would be easier. He would have to wait until the crops became ripe to harvest. Aditya pondered.

Chapter Thirteen

Kali left Aditya

What Daruk had told him earlier, was the truth. Indeed, the economic conditions of farmers were quite stable in Dharmkhet. Farmers were earning better than other professionals.

Aditya wanted to become a wealthy person very fast, and also needed his own house. From the day he had started earning, Daruk was receiving a portion of grains as the rent of his house. If Aditya had had his own abode for living, he could have utilized his entire earning for himself, thought Aditya.

Aditya prepared the soil using the techniques that he had learnt from other farmers, and sowed the seeds there, considering that he would become a rich person soon. Then he applied water to germinate the seeds.

The first step of the process of farming was completed, and he had not much work to do until the seedlings were coming out.

He went to Kaivartya, and said, "I've finished the work for today, and there is nothing much to do for me at this moment. Would you like to give me any unfinished work of yours?"

He said it with an intention. He was not going to work for free, but just wanted to earn further.

Vikranta could catch his intention, and he did not want to disappoint him.

He gently said, "Yes, I've a task for you. Inside my barn, you'll find a bullock which is too old to do work. It has no use now. I want to sell it, and buy a new one. Can you accomplish the task for me?"

"Obviously I can, if you direct me where I should go to sell it, and buy a young bullock."

"Wait here, I'm coming within a moment."

Kaivartya brought a bag with him, and said, "You should take the bullock, along with this bag containing the finest quality of herbs at the other bank of the river. There you find a person named Sunda, who is the only seller of all kinds of animals in Dharmkhet. You should buy a new bullock from him, exchanging the old bullock and this bag. After returning, you keep the young bullock at my barn. I hope you do this perfectly."

Kaivartya handed over the bag to him. Aditya opened a little to look inside. It contained several leaves, roots, dried fruits and flowers of some unknown plants.

Aditya asked in disappointment, "Would anyone agree to sell a new bullock exchange of these? It seems these are useless for someone to eat."

"You have no idea what kind of herbs those are. Those all have medicinal values. Sunda uses those herbs to cure several deadly diseases of animals."

Aditya was able to understand how valuable those herbs were. He did not ask more questions. Aditya carried the bag, and took out the oldest bullock from the barn, and set out for the journey. It was a long distance.

The river was narrow, and not much deep, yet its current was strong. He tightly held the collar rope of the bullock to keep it steady in the river water, and grabbed the bag at his chest with other hand. The water was streaming waist-high. Aditya became successful in crossing the river, but his dress became wet.

It was impossible for him to travel further wearing those wet clothes. His destination was five miles away from his location. He decided he should wait somewhere until his clothes became dry again.

He found an enormous banyan tree on the roadside, under which he could rest for a while, along with drying his clothes.

He tied the bullock to the tree, and put the wet clothes on its branches. Then he sat down under the tree leaning against its trunk.

A gentle breeze was blowing from the south, and whenever it touched his body, he was feeling sleepy. He closed his eyes, and did not know when he got asleep.

*****

Just before the sunset, a chewing sound of an animal's mouth made him awake. He realized that the day was almost over, and yet he had an unfinished task.

He stood up, and put on the dried clothes as fast as he could. Then picked up the bag from the ground, and received an unexpected shock. The bag was half empty. He looked at his surroundings to find out the person who could be responsible for the stealing. He found no one but the bullock, who was still chewing something in his mouth, and a piece of herbs was dangling from its lips.

He could understand the entire context. The bullock was the culprit for the undesirable situation of Aditya. He became furious at the bullock at once, and detached a suitable twig from the tree, and began to beat the bullock using his entire energy with the twig.

Aditya was beating the old bullock like a ruthless monster, and the bullock was unable to flee away as it was tied with the tree. The bullock was screaming in pain, but there was no one around to save the bullock from Aditya.

Aditya continued beating the bullock, and right at the moment he felt a sudden pain on his back along with a whoosh sound. The pain was so severe that he was unable to hold the twig for longer, and it fell down from his hand. It seemed that someone whipped him from behind. He turned around, and found no one there. Again someone whipped him, and fell on the ground in pain. An invisible person was whipping him continuously, and he was helpless to save himself. He realized the invisible person was none other than Vikranta.

"Why are you beating me that way? The bullock has stolen something, and was punishing it for the sin. Did you forget, you applied the same punishment when I was stealing fruits from someone's tree?"

The ghost stopped beating, and Aditya saw a beam of light in front of him. The light transformed into a human figure, and Aditya saw Vikranta was standing before him.

He was wearing a red colored hooded mantle, and a whip was hanging from his hand.

It was Vikranta then. But his face was not frightening at all, instead he looked like a god, thought Aditya.

"What an irony. A prince is now comparing himself with an animal. Your situation is really pathetic, I see," said Vikranta smiling.

Aditya was lying on the ground with tremendous pain. Still he had many questions that he wanted to ask Vikranta, but he asked the most obvious one.

"How do you know I was a prince?"

Vikranta smiled again. He said, "I know many things that a normal person can't imagine."

"And why did you beat me? Why didn't you beat the bullock for its sin?"

"Are you a child? Don't you know that the law of Karma is applicable only to humans? Being a human, you possess the sense of what is right and what is wrong. But since your childhood you have been always choosing wrong. So, you're considered to be a sinful person, and you have lost your true identity because of your Karma. You've no idea how precious getting a human life is, it's like a reward from god. God has given a chance to your soul to prove its divinity through your human life. If you fail to prove yourself, your soul has to be born into many lives as inferior creatures. Look at the bullock. I was born as a bullock because its soul failed to prove itself when it had lived as a human. Now that bullock has no capability to differentiate right and wrong. It has been going through a life of a bullock, and acting as a slave for humans. Would you like to be born as a bullock in your next life?" scolded Vikranta.

"No, I want to prove myself. I want to be human again in my next life."

"Every soul seeks its liberation, but you want a rebirth!"

"What is liberation?"

"It means getting freedom from all kinds of pain. A soul meets to its origin, the eternal being."

"I don't understand such philosophical talk. But, I'll try to differentiate good and bad from today, and choose the good one between the two," said Aditya, "But what should I do now? The bullock has eaten the herbs."

"It's not a problem at all."

Vikranta gestured his hand in the air, and the bag became full again by the magic."

"Why didn't you do the magic before? Then everyone could have avoided the punishment."

Vikranta threw a smile at him before disappearing from there.

At that moment Aditya felt his pain had gone away. His back was quite healed, and he was feeling good. He thought Vikranta had healed the pain before leaving. But he was wrong as he saw that a shadowy figure came out from his body, and stood in front of him.

"I can recognize you. We met before. You are Kali, who lives inside me."

Kali was covered with blood, and he was seemingly too weak to stand upright. His back was wounded with whipping scars. It seemed that he was suffering from the same pain, from which Aditya just got relief.

"You've recognized me correctly. I am Kali. I've been living inside your body from your beginning, I appeared myself to tell you today that I have to leave you now. I am very disappointed with your recent activities. You're becoming disobedient to me day by day, and it made me weaker. You can see, I'm so sick now that I am unable to stand steady. Nevertheless, you were my favorite host ever, but it's time to say goodbye."

"Now everything is clear to me. You are the evil demon who always compelled me to choose the wrong paths. You are responsible for all those sinful activities of mine, as well as the miserable fate of losing my identity was also the result of your evil action. Go away from here, and never return to me," scolded Aditya.

The demon Kali, along with its shadow went away from there, and Aditya felt free from an undesired evil bondage. He stepped close to the bullock, and gently put his hand on its back, and said, "I am sorry. Please forgive me."

Chapter Fourteen

The strange castle

Dusk was falling, but Aditya had travelled half of the distance from his destination. He was trying to move fast, but the bullock was unable to keep up with him due to its old age.

Aditya was quite sure that he would not be able to accomplish the task today. But, it would be bad, if Kaivartya kept on waiting for his return till the end of the night, thought Aditya.

He recalled the incident when he had met with the cart-puller. The cart-puller had refused to take him before informing his master regarding his absence at the workplace. He had told him that it was all about promise, and he was bound to keep his promise unbroken.

Had Aditya promised Kaivartya that he would accomplish the task within today? No he did not. Sometimes, a task needs more than one day to accomplish. But at present, he needed a longer time due to the effect of carelessness of himself.

Still, a logical interpretation told him that it would be nothing wrong if he did not accomplish the task today. Moreover, there was no moon in the sky, and it would be hard to see through the road properly in the darkness.

After thinking extensively, Aditya decided to spend the night somewhere nearby, and he would finish the undone task tomorrow morning. Also he would tell the entire incident to Kaivartya as an excuse, begging pardon from him.

Aditya began to think like a wise person, because Kali had lost control over him. It was obvious that, from now on, he would like to choose the righteous path to solve a problem.

Aditya looked around to find a shelter, where he could safely spend the night. Surprisingly the place was unambiguously deserted for an unknown reason, which was quite odd in Dharmkhet.

Aditya kept on walking, but there was no hut, no villager, and no other thing related to humankind. But after travelling a few steps more, Aditya found an extraordinary thing, which could not be believable to be seen in that territory. An enormous castle, and it was an ancient building.

Who had built a castle here? Dharmkhet was supposedly a place of a kind of people, who were leading their lives in poverty. How would someone build a castle like this? Aditya asked himself.

It seemed that the castle had been the abode of a royal family, but they were gone in history. Now it was covered with bushes, and wild plants. Its walls were cracked, and many parts of the castle were broken. Why did they not repair the castle? It could have been a better living place for several families.

Another interesting fact, which Aditya noticed, was that the castle was clearly visible in the darkness, yet it was not glowing. Mysteriously, an unexplainable property made the castle visible.

Aditya tied the bullock outside, and could not help, but entered the castle. There he encountered another mystery.

The interior was nicely decorated, and there was no sign of its ancientness. It was so neat and clean inside, as if someone was taking care of the castle regularly.

There were more astonishing things that made Aditya stunned entirely. Aditya found that each door of the castle was guarded by a pair of guards, and they were made of metals. Aditya performed a closer examination of those artifacts, and found those were sculpted brilliantly, as if soon they would come alive before his eyes.

Apart from those statues, there were many metallic things like, metallic utensils, idols, ornaments, and many uncountable numbers of metallic pieces that enhanced the attractiveness of the place. Most of them, including those statues were made of gold, and those were emitting a dim light that made everything visible in spite of darkness.

Suddenly Aditya discovered an interesting fact about Dharmkhet.

"Why didn't I notice it earlier?" scolded Aditya himself realizing the insufficiency of his intelligence.

Since the first day he had arrived here, he had not seen any single piece of metal in Dharmkhet. Even these people did not use any object which required metal to build. Such as, they did not use any kind of currency for buying things, because metal was necessary for manufacturing metallic coins. They did not use vehicles of any kind, because without use of metals, its structures would be fragile. They did not use any weapons, metallic utensils, even any metallic tools for regular usage. Aditya remembered, a few days ago he had found some ornaments in Daruk's wardrobe. Those were made of wood, instead of metal.

Aditya wondered why these people had chosen to stay in poverty abandoning the large amount of treasure. He should have to solve the mystery soon, decided Aditya.

Aditya entered another room. It could not be called a room at all, as it was a enormous hall, where a king usually sat on the throne, and solved the problems of the dwellers of his kingdom. Aditya found the throne at the front, along with several metallic artifacts, and metallic statues of soldiers. In the middle of the hall, he observed two golden statues of women. The elder woman was holding a beautiful necklace in her hand, and a teenage girl touched the hand of that woman. Probably these were the statues of a mother and her daughter.

Aditya looked at the teenage daughter, and she was beautiful indeed. If she were a real person, no girl in the world could be compared to her beauty, thought Aditya.

Aditya felt an attraction towards the girl statue. He wanted to hold her hand, despite it was metallic.

He stepped towards the girl, and was about to touch her hand. At that moment, suddenly he heard a loud voice.

"Leave the castle now. It's dangerous."

Aditya could recognize the voice. It was Vikranta. A while ago, he had encountered him, and now he appeared again in the front of the golden throne.

Sudden appearance of Vikranta made Aditya frightened.

He faltered, "I was.... I just.... I was just thinking villagers' poverty could be abolished if they used that enormous amount of treasure."

"What do you think, they don't know about it? But, they are not allowed to use these."

"But why?" asked Aditya curiously.

"If anyone touches metal of any kind, he'll be transformed into it."

"Then that's the reason why they do not use metals. Why is it so?" asked Aditya in extreme surprise.

"Because they are cursed. This place is cursed. And as soon as you entered in Dharmkhet, You're carrying the same curse too. You would transform yourself into a gold statue like them, if you touched the girl."

"That means they were alive once? They are not just statues?"

"Of course they were alive. These two women you can see, do you know who they are?"

"No," muttered Aditya.

"They are the wife and the daughter of Daruk. I hope you know Daruk very well?"

"Yes, I live in his home. But why don't you make them alive again, using your power?"

"It's not possible. Who had put the curse once, was not an ordinary person. He was pure evil."

"Who was he?"

"Kali, the demon."

"Yes, I know him. He lived inside me all the time without my knowledge. But today he left my body."

"Really? You can't imagine how happy I am after hearing that. It has to be, I knew it, because you are....."

Vikranta did not finish the sentence. He stopped suddenly while speaking to Aditya.

"What happened? Why did you stop?"

"No, nothing," answered Vikranta thoughtfully. He continued, "It's good for you then. That demon is unable to live inside anyone's in Dharmkhet. But he can live inside metals. As an outsider, you carried him in your body for a long period, but since you changed your character after coming here, he could not manage to stay inside of you."

Aditya suspected that Vikranta wanted to keep something secret from Aditya. He predicted it, watching Vikranta's body language. But he did not dare to ask that. Rather he asked, "Is there any possibility to make these people alive again?"

"It's only possible by eliminating the curse."

"How to eliminate the curse? Let me know."

"It's very hard. You'll come to know the procedure, when the proper time will come. Now you should leave the castle."

"But where do I stay tonight?"

"Stay anywhere, but not in this castle. Leave now," said Vikranta in a loud and echoing voice, and he disappeared.

Aditya came out from the castle, and took shelter under a tree. That night he could not sleep, but kept on thinking about the castle, about Kali, about the curse of Dharmkhet, and obviously about the girl statue, the daughter of Daruk. One time he could see a light in the eastern region of the sky. It was already dawn.

Chapter Fifteen

The story of Daruk

Aditya returned to his workplace before noon, and affirmed Kaivartya that he had successfully accomplished the task, presenting a young bullock before him. Also, he admitted that he had had a nap on the way because of his own fault, and there would be no repetition of the same in the future. But he did not mention Vikranta, or Kali, or the castle to him, thinking, those incidents were not related to the reason for his delay.

After returning to Daruk's home, he met Daruk and said, "I saw your wife and daughter yesterday night. They became gold statues."

"How do you know that? I didn't tell you before."

"Vikranta told me that," said Aditya. And then he described the entire happenings of yesterday. Daruk listened to him paying full attention, and when Aditya finished, Daruk said, "You've no idea how fortunate you are that Vikranta appeared before you. I wished to see him for once, but he didn't appear to me like that. Even a very few people got the chance to see him in their lifetimes. You are the luckiest person ever. You came here barely one month ago, and Vikranta appeared before you twice on the same day, just imagine. When my wife and daughter transformed into metal, I thought that Vikranta might be the only person who could make them alive again. I shouted at him many times looking at the sky, 'Please Vikranta, forgive her sins, and give their lives back.' But he never responded."

"Vikranta has no power to make them normal. He told me that. The place is cursed; all these villagers are cursed. They'll transform into metal if they touch it."

"I always thought that it was merely a myth. From our childhood our parents taught us that any kind of metal is the most unholy thing for us, and we should not touch metal. But when I saw that my family transformed into metal in front of my eyes, I realized, it was not a myth at all."

"Why did they go there? Didn't they know the myth?"

"Of course they knew. But don't blame my daughter for her mother's fault. She was not responsible at all. She just wanted to save her mother. But, at the moment when she touched her mother, she transformed into gold too."

"Please tell me the entire incident from the beginning. I'm just thinking how mysterious the place is," said Aditya thoughtfully.

"Alright then, I'm going to tell you the entire story of my life," said Daruk, and began his story.

*****

"I lived with my parents in Dharmkhet from my childhood, and I grew up here. My father was a farmer, and mother was a housewife. When I was a teenage boy, a girl arrived at Dharmkhet with her father. She was two or three years younger than me.

104

One day, while my father was busy in the field, cultivating crops, he saw a man who was lying under a tree, and her daughter was taking care of him. The man was nearly dying. Probably they were starving for a long period. My father had brought them to our home, and cured the man with proper medicines.

They had come from Kuru. Everyone knew that Kuru's ruler exiled the criminals through the long road leading to Dharmkhet. It has been happening since long before. But, astonishingly, Kuru's ruler has many times chosen the wrong person as a criminal. That man was not a criminal at all.

Gradually, my father and the person became good friends. Eventually they were unable to leave Dharmkhet, as the invisible wall surrounded the place. Few months later they built their own home, and lived in Dharmkhet permanently.

His daughter was a pretty girl. I made friends with her, and gradually the friendship changed into love. Her name was Sandhya."

"She was your wife, wasn't she?"

"Yes, after a certain age, we got married. One year later, Mitra was born."

"Her name was Mitra then," uttered Aditya.

"She was my daughter. The greatest gift from god that I received. My family was complete, and it could have been a happy family. But it was not," sighed Daruk.

"What happened then?" asked Aditya.

"I was not a farmer like my father. I chose my profession as a carpenter, and for that reason I was a poor person. On the other hand, I loved Sandhya very much, and I always tried to satisfy her by fulfilling all her demands. Probably she belonged to a wealthy family before. She was always attracted to the things which were precious, and she wanted the things that she liked. Day by day her desires were increasing, and I failed to fulfill most of them. My daughter also reached her teenage years, and she needed extra care than before, thus it was certainly impossible for me to keep my wife always happy.

One day, she said to me that she once saw an ornament on the queen's neck when she lived in Kuru. She wanted the same ornament from me. I asked her to draw a picture of that, so I could make it for her. She painted a beautiful drawing of that necklace, and it was golden. Sandhya was a good painter indeed. I decided that I would make the same with wood, and I carved wood at the level of my best, and made that necklace for her.

When it was finished, I presented the necklace to her, expressing love. She received it from my hand, and glimpsed at it carelessly, and at the next instance, she threw the necklace away.

I was shocked, and my heart was broken too, seeing her behavior. Still I asked her softly what had happened. She answered me rudely that It was not even close to what she had seen. The actual necklace was more bright, and shiny. I assured her that I would try once more, and make the same. But, I failed again. I kept on trying several times to make the same necklace for her, but she was not satisfied. Then she mentioned that the original necklace was made of gold.

I was stunned when she spoke the word 'gold'. She knew well that metals are forbidden for us, still she was demanding it.

I gently reminded her that metals are forbidden materials for us, and suggested, she should renounce that desire forever.

After listening to that, she gave me a strong reply. She declared in a sharp voice that she would not demand anything from me in the future."

Daruk's mouth was dried. He asked for water from Aditya. Aditya realized his mental condition. He poured some water into a bowl from the large clay pot, which was kept inside the room, and gave the bowl to Daruk.

Daruk drank the entire quantity of water, even the last drop of it, and started again, "She did so. From that day, she stopped asking for anything from me. It was a huge relief for me. I thought, from then on, I would be able to utilize my entire earnings in a good way. But her statement was more serious than I thought. I noticed a sudden change in her behavior. It seemed, all the happiness, which she possessed, was taken away. She talked very little to me, and she barely answered whenever I asked any questions regarding trivial household affairs. Even my daughter was feeling a deficiency of affection from her.

Her behavioral change worried me after a few days, and I began to blame myself realizing her condition. I could not express how much I felt the pain.

One day I decided that I would take my family on a trip, considering It might help to heal her depression, and the next morning, we set out for a journey. Astonishingly on that day she was behaving normally, as she used to behave before. Her smile was back in her lips, and the loveliness, which she had lost once, was there again. It made me happy again after a long period.

No doubt, the happiness of a family is the key to mental peace for a person. Everything is good in a person's life if he belongs to a happy family, but the opposite may ruin everything in his life.

That day we spent quality time together at the beach of that beautiful lake. My wife, Sandhya, cooked for us, and Mitra and I assisted her with pleasure, and we had our lunch in the afternoon. It was a perfect picnic on the lap of nature.

Before the sunset, we were preparing to return home. That time I noticed that Sandhya changed herself again. Her smile was gone, and she was behaving abnormally as usual. It worried me again, and I realized all my efforts just went in vain.

We were moving fast to reach our home by nightfall. It was a long distance, and we had to pass near the castle. While we were travelling through the road near the castle, my daughter Mitra suddenly called out, "Mother, where are you?" Then she asked me, "Where's my mother gone?"

I looked around to find her, and she was nowhere. There was no such place nearby for hiding except the castle. Sandhya knew well that the abandoned castle was the abode of Vikranta, and no one should enter there. But yet I don't know what kind of force compelled her to take there. I rushed towards the castle, and Mitra was also running. She was running faster than me, and eventually she entered the castle before me.

When I finally found them, I saw that Sadhya was already transformed into a gold statue, and a beautiful golden necklace was in her hand. And my daughter, Mitra touched her hand, and before my eyes, Mitra was also transforming into gold. Her face was yet to be transformed into metal, and that moment, she spoke the last word to me, "Pitasree (father)."

I was a helpless father, and a husband. I had nothing to do but cry."

Daruk started crying. Aditya could not find any word to console him. Few moments later he continued again, "I prayed to Vikranta again and again to give their lives back, but he did not respond.

From that day, I realized the truth. The truth is that all the unhappiness in our lives originates from desire. Thus, desire is the main enemy of humans. My wife and my daughter would have stayed with me today, if my wife could renounce her desire. From that nightmarish day, I vowed that I would renounce all my desires, and then on, I became a desire-less person.

Still, I am unable to leave one particular desire, that is, if any miracle happens, and they get back their lives."

Aditya said, "I can understand your mental sufferings. No consolation is able to heal it. Still you should not blame your wife for her ignorance. I can find an intimate connection between that evil demon, and all those activities of your wife. That evil demon must have possessed your wife too."

"Who is the evil demon? Tell me everything."

"His name is Kali, an evil demon. Vikranta told me that he had put the curse on Dharmkhet. Not only that, I met that evil twice, and he left my body yesterday, just before I entered the castle. If he still remained inside me, I would have been a metal statue too, like your family. Since I was free from his evil power, I was able to control my greed after seeing an enormous amount of treasure inside the castle. Vikranta indeed saved my life yesterday. I am really grateful to him."

"I don't understand why the demon lived inside your body, or my wife's body. And what is the relation between the curse on Dharmkhet and him?"

"Vikranta yet didn't reveal the answers of those questions, but he has shown me hope."

"What kind of hope Aditya? Let me know, did Vikranta reveal any way how my family would get their lives back?" asked Daruk excitedly.

"No, but he has hinted to me that it would be possible somehow."

"Tell me Aditya how. I can do anything to make them alive."

Daruk was sobbing.

Aditya answered softly, "He only said, the procedure is difficult, but we will come to know it when the time will come in our favor."

Chapter Sixteen

Work without desire

Aditya gazed at the field covered with ripe crops. Those were dancing and flattering in the breeze.

Aditya marveled at the wonder of nature. A few months ago, when he had planted some tiny seeds on the ground, their true identities remained hidden inside themselves. But one-day morning, the seeds were germinated revealing their tiny leaves, and those newborn plants grew up with time under proper nourishment of farmers. After that, the leaves turned yellow, and now, they became ready for harvesting.

Most of the people might not find any strangeness in that entire cycle, because they considered the fact as a normal phenomenon without craving for its deeper insight. If they thought further, they would find it as a great magic shown by nature. How could a plant hide itself inside a tiny seed? Aditya asked himself.

"It's magnificent, isn't it?"

A voice coming from behind distracted his thoughts. Aditya turned around, and saw, Kaivartya was standing there.

Aditya stood up showing him respect, and said, "Indeed it's beautiful. I was thinking of the same. In fact, I was thinking of something more than that."

"What were you thinking, Aditya? Would you like to share with me if it's not associated with your personal life."

"I was just thinking about the unexplained sorcery of nature. Nature is continuously performing several incredible activities all the time that we are barely able to understand their secrets. These crops which we are seeing today, once they were hidden inside tiny seeds. If we look closely into the matter, we find, each plant also contains the similar kind of seeds, from which it was born. If we collect them, and sow them again, there will be more plants. It seems like an endless cycle. That way, if we could go back in time, we might have found one single seed which was the mother of all these plants. And we can conclude that nature had secretly hidden an ocean of plants inside that mother seed."

"What you've said is quite sensible. Most acts of nature are full of mystery. In spite of that, we are able to explain some of these. For example, you believe that all these crops had been shrunk inside the seeds, but reality is not such."

"Then what? I've just said what I observed."

"You observe an illusion created by nature, and she uses her own equipment to show it. We are not able to explain how she had made her equipment, but how her equipment behaves, we can explain. Let me clear your doubts about the seeds. Those seeds, and the five elements, air, fire, water, earth, and space are her equipment. When a seed is brought under a balanced environment of the five elements, the seed begins to accumulate these elements in its body. As a result, it germinates, starts growing. After a certain period, the plant realizes to keep its existence forever, and so, it makes several copies in the form of seeds, and after that the plant dies."

"I knew that. It's true for any living organism. But plants have no life."

"Who said that? Trees and plants are living organisms too, just like us. The only difference is that they are unable to move like animals."

"That mean they take food like us?"

"Of course they eat. They use their roots and leaves to take food. Their roots absorb soluble materials from the ground along with water. Due to this reason, we often apply water to them. And their leaves absorb air and light. So we plant them in a place where the combination of the five elements is perfectly balanced. If we nourish them with our utmost devotion, they will produce more grains. It is a kind of rule in our lives that if you get something, first you have to invest in something."

Aditya was listening to Kaivartya like an obedient student. At that moment, he asked the obvious question, which came to mind, "I've taken care of them, with my good efforts, just like other farmers did. Yet I can see that these plants didn't return me well. They've yielded very poor quantities. Why did they disappoint me that way?"

"Did you cultivate the crops with a wise mind?"

"Let me know first, what had been in your mind while you were farming."

"I was thinking like a good investor. I was aiming at how many months it would take to make me rich if I continued farming that way."

"That was the reason why you've failed to produce a sufficient amount of crops. You were thinking about the result before accomplishing the job."

"Why shouldn't I? People always do work to get good results."

"You are wrong. A result might be good or bad. But during the performance, if someone became too excited predicting a good result, or too depressed predicting a bad result, it would affect his performance, and at the end the result would be always undesirable. You have made the same mistake. If you sincerely devoted yourself to your job, without thinking about its outcome, you would have got a better result."

"We should work aimlessly then?" said a confused Aditya.

"No, you misunderstood me. Aim is a good thing in life. But, if you keep on thinking about your aim all the time, it will affect you unwittingly. And suppose you failed to achieve your goal, it would lead you to an intolerable depression at the end. So the rule is, always do work giving your extreme effort. You may achieve success, or failure after accomplishment of that work, but if you follow the rule, you will never lose enthusiasm in your life."

Aditya was in an intense wonder after cogitating the entire idea delivered by Kaivartya. He said, "I'll always

obey the rule in the future, and never repeat the same
mistake again."

Chapter Seventeen

Two years later

Two years had passed, and Aditya's personality had a significant change in that period. It was hard to believe that he was the same Aditya who had once been an aggressive, cruel, selfish, and arrogant prince. He became a person possessing politeness, kindness, and selflessness in his character.

It had not happened like instantaneous magic, rather it was a consequence of several moments that he had gone through. Just after his arrival at Dharmkhet, he had to maintain a good character due to the fear of Vikranta. But, as time went on, he met new people who were completely free from the evil effect of Kali, and it had helped a lot to improve his character subconsciously.

Kaivartya had played a major role in it. Along with farming, he also had delivered knowledge about moral values, and how he should apply them in his life. Also, he achieved success as a farmer following the lessons that he had learnt from Kaivartya.

Few months ago Aditya had built his own house, and lived there. Although he owned a house, and left Daruk's abode, he maintained a good relation with him like a father and a son.

Most of the days, he remained busy at his workplace, but a few days were different, when he could spend the days as vacations. He found a place beside the lake where he usually spent his vacation staying lonely.

He could have spent the vacations enjoying with other people, but he preferred to stay alone. No doubt his loneliness originated from the mental sufferings that he was bearing for his past mistakes.

Another activity he usually did on the holidays. He did not tell anyone yet about it, even, he was quite confused whether it was a sinful act or not. If it was a sin, why did Vikranta not punish him yet? He asked the question to himself many times, and found no answer. Then he decided it was not a sin.

Still he felt guilty whenever he repeated the act for the next time, and along with that, he also felt a sensation of romance.

It was all about a golden statue. The statue of Daruk's daughter, Mitra. Whenever he could manage some time from his holiday schedules, he visited the castle to see her. He always felt a strong attraction to her face. She was extraordinarily beautiful, and her face had a capacity to addict Aditya. Recalling her face gave him comfort, and healed the mental pain instantly for a certain period.

But Aditya frequently experienced a strange problem whenever he wanted to recall her. He was unable to capture the exact picture of her face in his mind, and for that reason, her face did not come again on his mental canvas when he tried to recall her.

He felt no problem recalling the face of his father, or recalling the faces of other people of Kuru, even though he could recall the faces of Samhati, and Vikarna. Not only that, he was able to recall the face of the cart puller too. But he always failed to recall Mitra's face. Aditya could not find any suitable reason why he always forgot her face. Maybe, the extreme beauty of her was not allowing him to be captured by him, giving him a persistent picture inside his mind for a long period. So he had to visit the castle again to restore her face in his memory.

Aditya knew the sensation, which he was feeling, people called it love, but whenever people would come to know about it, they would begin to call it madness. Aditya decided, if ever that girl would get her life back, he would spend his life with her.

*****

On a nice holiday afternoon, Aditya was sitting under an enormous rosewood tree on the top of a mountain cliff, from where he was able to get an extensive view of the entire lake, the mountains, the waterfall, and the magnificent scenery of their surroundings. It was a moment for recalling the past. More appropriately, he was trying to criticize his wrong actions that he had committed before.

It was obvious that he was not solely responsible for those sinful acts, as the evil demon Kali had always misguided him. However, Aditya had the free choice of accepting the righteous path over the wrong, but the demon wanted that Aditya should choose the wrong one.

Aditya could have fought against Kali's will through controlling himself, but he failed to do so. If he had had proper guidance from someone who would teach him the distinction between good and bad, all the misfortunate incidents could have been avoided, thought Aditya.

The village Dharmkhet was truly mysterious. There was no influence of Kali. It seemed that Kali lost all his power here. Eventually, Vikranta had told him once the same. As Kali was unable to control over people, they lived here with happiness, in spite of having extreme poverty. Moreover, their minds were so pure that they hardly performed any sinful act.

Still, they were unable to get a true rescue from Kali. Kali had taken away a useful facility from them that they were not allowed to touch any metal.

All the mysteries still remained unsolved. How were the dwellers of Dharmkhet consistently maintaining good characters? And why was the entire territory enclosed by an invisible wall? People believed that Vikranta had built the wall for their good, and he was keeping them away from any sin. But, if Vikranta was considered to be a good soul, why would he punish innocent people by confining them with a wall? Definitely, something strange was going on in Dharmkhet, thought Aditya.

What was the history of the castle? And what was the identity of Vikranta, when he had lived as a human?

Aditya had too many unanswered questions, but the most important question, which Aditya asked to himself was related to his life. Would he ever be able to get back his past life? Or, would he have to spend the rest of his life in Dharmkhet as a farmer?

Once Vikarna's soul had revealed a way how Aditya would be able to eliminate the curse. But he was still unsure whether Vikarna's had appeared to him in reality, or it had been a kind of illusion that he had experienced in the state of sickness. If he considered that the incident had happened in reality, it would be still difficult for Aditya to fulfill the condition, which could eliminate the curse.

What was the condition that Vikarna's soul had set? Aditya recalled it from the past. He would have to accept the present life willingly. He would have to believe that the present life as an ordinary villager would be better than the past life as a prince.

Would it even be possible?

If it would not be possible, why had Vikarna made such a condition?

He would ask Vikarna if he would come to him again, thought Aditya.

"Do you remember me, Aditya?"

An unexpected voice, which was calling by Aditya's name, sought his attention. Who could be the person who found Aditya in this tranquil place where he usually spent his time alone? He turned around, and found Vikarna, who was standing a few steps away from him.

"Is it real? Or, is it an illusion created by my mind due to excessive thinking?" asked Aditya thoughtfully.

"Of course, it is real. As real as you have been experiencing all those incidents during the years in Dharmkhet," replied the soul.

"How do you know what I've experienced in recent years?"

"Because I have been with you, and watching your activities throughout the time. I've seen how you have changed yourself into a person of a different kind. I witnessed the entire process of change hiding myself from your vision."

"It's true, and I can also feel the change within me. Now I have deep repentance for those actions, which I did in the past. It was utterly unlawful, what I did to you on the battlefield. I am not a person who deserves mercy from you, yet I want to beg it from you. Please forgive me, Vikarna, for all those mistakes from me," cried Aditya.

"I have already forgiven you at that moment, when you started to realize your past sins. Right now, I do not possess any anger, or mentality of vengeance against you. I can believe now, my soul will find peace one day, realizing that it became the reason for someone's betterment."

"Your words gave me relief to some extent. I have no capacity to rectify my past actions. Nevertheless, I can console myself, considering that our enmity has ended."

"It satisfies me as well. However, I feel a little pain inside me seeing that you are still suffering from the curse, and I am unable to help you regarding its abolition. Since you were given the capacity to eliminate it, no other person can help you. It is like a battle, and you have to fight against your own mind to win the battle."

"I have been thinking the same. I was searching for a way how the curse could be eliminated, but it confused me every time. It is utterly impossible for me to accept a bad thing over good. How can I willingly choose an ordinary lifestyle, forgetting my past identity?"

"What is good, and what is bad? Isn't it apparent from human to human? Just think about yourself. Once you believed that the actions, which you did before, were good, and now you are realizing those were bad. What do you think, Aditya? Do you really believe that your present life is less worthy than the past? If your answer is 'yes', tell me the reason why?"

"Because I'm missing my father badly, and..."

"And?" asked Vikarna's soul, as Aditya paused for a moment while continuing the sentence.

"And..." muttered Aditya again, and suddenly realized that he was unable to find any plausible reason to answer.

Once he believed that lazy people are quite happy as they do not work. Following the principle, Aditya used to avoid doing work, and had kept several servants to solve his purposes. But now he discovered, doing something is better than doing nothing, and he kept himself busy at work to stay happy.

Once he had been able to get anything precious according to his need, but that precious thing lost its value near Aditya soon after he achieved it. Now he knew, anything could be precious for someone, when the person spent a good effort to earn the thing.

When he had been a prince, he possessed an enormous amount of wealth, but now he knew, any amount of wealth could be sufficient to satisfy an uncontrolled desire.

Finding no suitable answer, after thinking for a while, Aditya finished the sentence in a hurry, "And, I used to be a prince."

"Very strange!" said Vikarna, "You're finding this life is worthless just because you're missing your father, and the term prince is sounding very sweet? It seems that you've wisely accepted many aspects of this life, which you once considered as deficient. You have to admit the fact, Aditya, that you wouldn't change your perceptions about things, if you did not go through a series of unfortunate events in your life."

Aditya had nothing to say, as he began to realize what Vikarna was saying was quite meaningful.

Vikarna continued, "Every incident that happened in the past, or is happening in the present, or will happen in the future, regardless of the fact it's good or bad, has had a purpose. It maintains a balance of the universe. If everything were good, the term 'bad' never existed, there would be no darkness in the presence of immense brightness, night never came as daytime would persist forever, and there would be no winter due to the presence of a never ending spring. All these are seemingly sounding like a paradise. But if the universe went on that way, after a certain period, it would create an imbalance in nature, which might have been the reason for an unwanted apocalypse. So, nature adopted itself in such a way that bad and good can come and go periodically. It is also true for every human life. Everyone is obliged to experience good times and bad times for a certain period in his life. No one can escape from that. Although the curse delivered you extreme sufferings, in the end you've changed yourself into a better human being due to its beneficial effects."

"I do agree with everything that you've said. Still, why did you have to leave the world so early. Why wasn't I?"

"Maybe my time had ended, and the universe conspired to make you stay alive for a better reason, which might not have been possible if I would live today."

"What could be the reason?" asked Aditya.

"It's still unknown to me. But I am quite sure you will discover the reason very soon."

*****

Vikranta's soul had gone from there a while ago, and Aditya kept on iterating the entire conversation over and over in his mind, as it was not easy for him to assimilate a new concept so quickly.

Bad are not actually bad then, instead those are maintaining a good balance. It provides a thrust to keep the universe stable.

It should have a deeper meaning. He had been under control of the evil demon, Kali for a purpose then, Aditya thought. Not only that, the reason for the existence of that evil had a purpose too?

As Aditya was thinking extensively, it was puzzling him more. He decided that he should find the answer later.

But what would happen to the curse? Would it be eliminated soon? Was it still persisting just because he loved his father so much? If he could forget his father, the curse would have gone away. But it was impossible to forget a person whom he loved.

Loving someone is an eternal entity. A love cannot be forgotten, but it can be compensated by another love. He should have to search for a person who would be able to compensate for his father's love.

At that moment, a thought came into his mind about Mitra's statue. She could have been a substitute, if she lived today.

"Oh, how beautiful she is. God created her in a perfect way. Her face is so innocent. It is a face that has no trace of sin."

Aditya tried to visualize her face in his mind, but he could not. Whenever he tried to recall her face, many faces came there, but no one matched her. Everytime, he failed to recall her properly. It was a great wonder to him.

Aditya whispered, "I'm coming Mitra to see you again. This time I'll preserve your beauty forever, and keep on recalling you, whenever I want."

Chapter Eighteen

The scion of Kuru

There was ample time before sunset. Aditya estimated, if he spent a few hours inside the castle, it would not be a big deal.

Aditya arrived at the castle on time. As usual the interior of the castle was dark, even in the daytime. Still the mysterious luminescence emitting from the statues made everything visible.

He entered the hall where Mitra and her mother stood in the same gestures like always. Finally, it gave Aditya a gentle breeze of comfort. Now he was able to see her face again. An exact illustration of that face, which had disappeared from his mental canvas due to a long separation, now recovered again.

How could the life of a beautiful young girl like Mitra be ruined that way? It would be an incurable suffering for Aditya, if she would remain as a gold statue during her lifetime, thought Aditya.

He uttered in his mind, "Look at her eyes, those are like a pair of blossoming lotus in a lake. Her eyebrows enhance their beauty. Her lips shaped perfectly, similar to a bow. Her figure was perfect, as it has been carved by the greatest artist in the world. Why has this art lost its life? It could be a mistake done by nature. Why would nature want her instability, destroying her own art? Nature has certainly made a mistake."

Aditya had to stop uttering as he suddenly heard a sound of footsteps coming inside the castle.

"Who could come here in this wrong place? Everyone knows the castle is a forbidden place for villagers."

Aditya followed the footsteps quietly hiding himself in another room. A few moments later, it stopped, and he could hear a conversation between two people. He recognized both of the voices. Without any doubt, the first one was Vikranta, the ghost. And if he was not making any mistake, the second one was Kaivartya. Aditya peered through the door hiding himself behind a wide column, to see his face. Indeed, Kaivartya was there.

"Why did he come here?" asked Aditya himself.

The conversation was going on, and Aditya kept on listening to it, standing on his spot.

"Welcome Kaivartya. I have been looking for you since this morning," said Vikranta.

"I beg your pardon my lord. I would have come earlier, but one of my bullocks strayed away in the morning, and I had to spend a few hours searching for it."

"No need for an explanation. I already know it. Do you forget, I keep my eyes open always to watch what is going on in Dharmkhet."

"I know my lord. You are one who protects the place and its people from eradication. If you were not here, the entire place would not exist."

"It was my duty, Kaivartya. That place belonged to me when I used to be a king, and I was responsible for all their sufferings. I had lost all hopes after my death, but it was your forefather, Satvik, who had given me strength. He had promised me that whenever I need any assistance, his heirs will assist me. I spent many days in uncertainty about his promise. I feared what would happen if Satvik's heirs refused to do the job. But every heir of Satvik, including you, did their duty with dedication. Now my perception has changed. I believe that we are on the right track, and everything is going to be normal like before. It has been more than thousand years that people of Dharmkhet has been suffering from the curse, and along with that, I am also suffering from my life as a spirit. Until the curse is intact, I am unable to achieve my liberation. The expected moment is very near, and for that reason, I am grateful to every heir of Satvik, especially to you. If you were unsuccessful in improving his character, we would lose our last hope."

"I am fortunate that I got the opportunity to do something good for our land, Dharmkhet. All the dwellers of Dharmkhet consider the land as their mother. Any of them would do the same. But, coincidentally my forefather had sworn to you in history, and I am bound to return his debt."

"Whenever I see you, it refreshes the memory of Satvik. I find his shadow within you. You got the same behaviour that he had possessed. Now tell me, Kaivartya, what do you think, is the boy ready yet to perform such an action?"

"I think so. I've noticed a drastic change in him. He wisely accepted Dharma, renouncing all those bad qualities which he had possessed once."

"I've noticed it too, and I believe that the perfect time has come to tell him about the true history that was forgotten by people."

"It's a good decision, I would say. I'll send him here tomorrow morning."

"You have not to. He's already present here," said Vikranta, and he turned up his voice, "Aditya, I know you are here, now reveal yourself."

Aditya got a tremendous shock when Vikranta called him. Thus, during the conversation the mentioned boy was none other than Aditya.

Apart from the state of astonishment, it was a moment of embarrassment for Aditya. As he would have to explain the reason for his presence in this abandoned castle.

An embarrassed and confused Aditya came out from behind the column making a bewildered face.

"Aditya, you are here! What are you doing here?" asked Kaivartya in astonishment.

"I.... I...."

Aditya found no answer to give. He was feeling guilty, in spite of having no guilt.

Vikranta managed the situation. He said to Kaivarta, "It would be better if you don't ask the reason, because the reason is related to his private life. Moreover, it is not a suitable moment for asking him any question, as he is already confused."

Then he turned to Aditya, and said something that created more confusion in him, "What I am going to tell you is hard to believe, but true. You and I belong to the same bloodline."

"I can't understand," said Aditya.

"Thousand years ago, I used to be a member of the Kuru family, just like you."

"How?" asked Aditya.

Then Vikranta described to him an incredible history, which brought goosebumps to Aditya's arms.

Chapter Nineteen

A thousand years old story

When Mahakaal, the god of time, had created time, he had felt the necessity of its division to maintain a perfect balance of the universe. He divided time into four categories. Those were termed as Yugas.

He employed four celestial beings to rule the world during the timeline of each Yuga.

The first yuga was called Satya, and its name was derived from the first celestial being having the same name. The characteristics of Satya Yuga matched accordingly with its name. Satya means truth, and the celestial person, who had ruled that time, possessed a pure character of divinity. Thus Satya Yuga was pure, truthful, and divine in nature. No evil was allowed to show its effect in that Yuga.

The second Yuga was known as Treta, and it got its name from the second celestial person, Treta, who possessed two third part divine, and one third part demonic character. Thus Treta Yuga had one third evil qualities.

Likewise, Dwapara, the third Yuga had increased its evil, and possessed equal amounts of evil and divine qualities.

All those incidents of Mahabharata had happened during the twilight of Dwapara. Dwapara had an end, and the upcoming Yuga, Kali was trying to invade the world.

The celestial being representing the fourth Yuga, Kali, was a demon. At first he possessed the elder Kaurava, Durjyadhana. As a result, Durjyadhana became a person of evil qualities like a demon. Although he was a human being, his personality did not match with a human, and he had done several sinful activities like a demon throughout his lifetime. It was a matter of distress that the great battle of Kurukshetra was the result of his wickedness.

However, Dwapara was still in action, and at the end of the war, good won, and evil lost. Kali became unsuccessful in conquering the world at that time.

Five Pandava brothers were still alive, and along with them, lord Krishna was the ultimate barrier in Kali's intention. Kali understood that he would have to wait a few years more.

A few decades later, one day lord Krishna passed away.

After the death of Krishna, Pandavas decided that they should leave Hastinapur, as their time had ended too. On a certain day, they left Kuru, and set out for the great journey, Mahaprasthan, renouncing all the royal comforts.

Before leaving Kuru, Yudhisthir handed over the entire kingdom to the grandson of Arjuna, Parikshit. It was a good scope for Kali to show his powers. All the obstacles on his path were eliminated, and Parikshit was a seemingly weak king compared to his grandfather Yudhisthir. He was not able to resist Kali's evil powers.

Once Parikshit visited the rural areas of his kingdom to observe how well people are leading their lives there. While travelling along the country road, he encountered a person who was mercilessly beating a handicapped ox on the roadside.

He prevented the man forcefully, and said, "How dare you commit such an atrocious act in my kingdom? Now be ready for a punishment."

"Pardon my king, I was not committing any crime. This ox is not letting me stay here. Until he leaves, I'm unable to stay. So, I just wanted to expel him from the place," said the man.

"I can't understand what kind of excuse you're showing. It's utterly impossible for a handicapped ox to occupy your place against your wish. Tell me the actual truth," scolded the king.

The man revealed the truth, "Alright, I'm going to tell you the truth. Neither the ox is ordinary, nor I. I'm Kali, and according to the laws of nature, the present time is mine. I have been finding a place to stay, but Dharma, who's disguised himself into an ox, is continuously resisting me, and is not letting me stay."

Parikshit considered that the man was insane. He asked annoyingly, "Will you release the ox if I provide a suitable place for your living?"

"Why not? I badly need an abode."

"Name a place then. Tell me, where do you want to live?"

"Gold seems to be a suitable place for me. I want to stay inside gold."

Parikshit stared at him spellbound. But he could not keep on staring for long as his face was very ugly. Considering his demand as his madness, he just answered, "I am allowing you. You can stay."

Parikshit wanted to say something, but before he could say, the man and the ox disappeared from the spot.

After a few moments, Parikshit felt tired, as he had travelled a long distance. He was thirsty too, and needed water to drink.

Travelling a few steps more, he found a hermitage. It was the hermitage of a sage, known as Shamik.

He entered the hermitage, and observed the sage was in a state of deep meditation sitting under an enormous banyan tree. He did not find any other person there except the sage.

Parikshit stepped slowly near the meditating sage, and said, "Please give me some water."

The sage did not answer any, as he was so deeply engaged in meditation that he was unable to hear any sound.

The king turned up the voice, "Give me some water. I am thirsty."

Still, there was no answer.

Then Parikshit brought rudeness in his voice, and said annoyingly, "I need water. Why are you not listening to me? Are you deaf?"

The meditating state of Shamik remained intact. There was no noticeable movement in his body.

The demon began to show his actions altering the king's mind towards evil. Since Parikshit was wearing a gold crown, Kali got an opportunity to overpower his mind.

Parikshit found a dead snake lying beside the tree. He removed an arrow from the quiver, and lifted the dead snake from the ground with its tip, and put the snake on the shoulder of the sage.

Meanwhile, the sage's son returned the hermitage from somewhere, and watched that the king was performing an atrocious act on his father.

It was indeed intolerable for a son to watch that his father was being dishonoured by a person before his eyes.

Sage Shamik's son, whose name was Shringi, put a curse upon the king saying, "You have done an immoral act, and dishonored my father when he was supposedly unconscious in his meditating state. It goes against the rule of Dharma. So I curse on you that your death will happen within seven days by snake bite."

After the incident, he returned to the castle feeling ashamed, for what he had done, and confined himself in a cabin, which had no window or hole, from where a snake could enter.

He spent six days that way. There was no possible way, by which he would have to die by snake bite. He thought, if anyway he could successfully spend the seventh day, the curse would be proven wrong.

Several kinds of fruits were kept in the room for his survival. While thinking the curse had been almost proven wrong, he picked up an apple from the plate, and took a gentle bite.

Suddenly he observed a small caterpillar was peering from the bitten portion of the apple. King Parikshit was scared. He threw the half bitten apple on the ground. The next moment, he watched that the caterpillar began to grow its size, and within a few moments, it transformed itself into a venomous snake.

Before Parikshit could realize what was happening, the snake bit on his leg.

The venom spread all over his body, and made him bluish. That way, Parikshit fell on the lap of death, and ended his life.

On the next day when people discovered his dead body, they found the venomous snake too. They tried to kill the snake, but it fled away.

*****

After the death of Parikshit, his elder son Janmejya became the next emperor of Kuru. Just after Janmejya availed the power of the throne, he vowed that he would destroy all the snakes from the earth.

According to the decision, he arranged a special kind of Yagna, which was known as Sarpasatra, that would fetch the snakes from every corner of the earth, and throw them into the ignited fire.

During the Yagna, Janmejya successfully killed almost half of the population of snakes, but if he destroyed the entire population, it would result in an adverse effect to the ecosystem created by nature.

A young sage, named Aastik convinced him to stop such an atrocious act.

*****

That part of the story was written in history, but a forgotten part of the history had never been told. Perhaps people had thought that it deserved lesser importance.

I am going to describe to you that forgotten part, which was related to Dharmkhet.

The great king of Kuru, Parikshit had two sons. I am Vikranta, who used to be the younger son of Parikshit, and brother of Janmejya.

Since I was the younger son, after my father's death, I became the ruler of a small part of Kuru, which was Dharmkhet.

Dharmkhet was not like today. Its area was quite large and prosperous. By any means, that Dharmkhet could be compared with today's Dharmkhet.

The death of my father made me depressed. Just like my elder brother Janmejya, I sought vengeance too. However, the execution of Sarpasatra had given me a mental relief, thinking that my brother, Janmejya, would now be able to appease my fathers's soul.

But Janmejya disappointed me. When I came to know that he had ceased the Yagna (Sarpasatra) after receiving the request from an unknown sage, the craving for vengeance rose inside me again.

I could have continued the Sarpasatra considering it an unfinished act of my brother, but I thought in a different way. It sounded mysterious to me that my father had received a curse and died because he had performed an action which was unlikely to be matched with his personality. I decided that I should first discover the reason for my father's misbehavior.

I arrived at Hastinapur to investigate the reality.

No one had any idea about that incident that he had encountered with Kali before visiting Shamik's hermitage. I preferred to ask my brother if he could tell me why my father had behaved abnormally on that day. But, just like other people, he had no idea. Still, he suggested to me that sage Shamik might know the reason better.

I went to sage Shamik's hermitage considering that he might give me any clue.

I asked the sage, showing him respect, "Maharshi (the great sage), my father, king Parikshit, left the earth a few days ago, as he received a curse from your son. He got the punishment because he dishonoured you once. After the death of my father, I am going through an extremely remorseful situation. It saddened me all the time, whenever I asked myself why my father performed a wrongful act. As I knew him, expecting such an action from him was impossible. So, I come to you to find an explanation behind such an abnormal behavioral change of my father."

"I am also saddened after getting the news of our beloved king's death. His behavioral change had surprised me as well. When I came to know he received a curse from my son, I was sure that the wrong person received the curse. Possibly a very strong force had enchanted him at the moment when he put a dead snake on my shoulder," said the Sage.

It sounded impossible to me, so I asked him, "What kind of force was that? How could a minor evil take control over my father?"

"Maybe that evil force was stronger than his willpower. Much stronger than we can imagine."

"Can you tell me about the force?"

"An evil force always needs an ordinary object, through which it becomes able to show its effect. If you really want to know about it, I have to examine his costume, which he had worn that day."

The sage came to my brother's castle, and carefully examined my father's clothes, his sword, his bow and arrows, the quiver, his shoes, and other things, but found nothing evil there.

I informed him that my father was wearing one more thing that day, which was the royal crown. At that moment, the crown belonged to my brother.

I brought the crown to him after asking it from my brother, and when he touched the crown, he received a tremendous shock.

"It's Kali!" screamed the sage.

"Who is Kali?" I asked him surprisingly.

"It is Kali, the demon, he has returned, and it is impossible to get rescue from his evil grasp."

Then he informed me everything about the demon. How he returns after a certain period of time, and how my father had permitted him to take shelter in gold.

Day by day, Kali would become more powerful. At first it had contaminated gold, and after that, it would contaminate other metals too. And thereafter, it would contaminate everything on the earth. That way, the demon would spread the evil poisoning human minds.

I ask him for any remedy that could stop him. He answered, no power on earth would be able to stop him.

Chapter Twenty

Metal is dangerous

With lost hope, I returned to my own castle at Dharmkhet. Still a craving for the vengeance resided inside me all the time. One year passed, and I had to watch helplessly how people were changing their character before my eyes. The initial effect could be noticed among the goldsmiths. Those goldsmiths, who once had been honest at their businesses, recently started stealing gold from the ornaments of their customers.

No other person, except me, was able to realize the seriousness about what had been going on in Dharmkhet. Apart from goldsmiths, other people were also changing their characters, and I was aware that it was the beginning of Kali Yuga. Soon the demon would transform the world into garbage. However, I decided, I should protect my Dharmkhet from the adverse effects of Kali applying all my abilities.

I imposed total prohibition on gold in Dharmkhet. No one would be allowed to use gold, and they should submit all their golden objects at the castle, in return, they would receive an equal amount of money worth of the gold.

I stopped using gold in manufacturing coins, in ornaments, and all other purposes. After that step, I noticed positive changes among people, but not for a longer period.

Kali started affecting other metals too, and I had to stop him before the situation would become out of control.

I banned all kinds of metals in Dharmkhet. Such a decision was quite difficult to apply as metallic objects were necessary things in their daily lives. They had to abandon the use of any metal in utensils, ornaments, furniture, and other necessary things for their basic needs. Even I stopped using any currency in my kingdom, as metal was a necessary thing for manufacturing coins. Instead, we started the custom of exchanging things to buy things.

But a complete ban on metal was not possible, because weapons were necessary instruments to protect our kingdom from invaders, for that reason, I allowed the use of metal among the soldiers, and other royal guards.

Soon after the ban, poverty broke out in Dharmkhet as an adverse effect. I became worried after seeing the financial condition of my people, yet I got satisfaction thinking that Kali was now unable to poison their minds, and due to that reason, they would stay happy even in their poor conditions.

It was not a good solution to the problem. How could people refrain themselves from using metal for their lifetime? I sought for a permanent solution, and ten years later, I accidentally met Satvik.

I had been so busy ruling my kingdom that I had not seen my brother for more than a decade. After all, Hastinapur used to be my old abode where I had spent my childhood.

One morning I took my horse, and set out towards Kuru to see my brother, Janmejya, and to observe how effectively he had been protecting the dwellers of Kuru from the evil grasp of Kali.

But I could not accomplish what I decided, because my destiny did not allow me. Riding my horse, while I was directed towards Kuru along the long dusty road, I needed to take a sudden halt, as I saw a man who was lying in the middle of the road.

"Is he dead?" I asked myself.

Climbing down from the horse, I stepped near him.

He looked like a sage, as I noticed. He was a young man wearing a saffron cloth, and his hair, and beard were long, which was similar to the characteristics of a sage. He barely had any flesh in his body, as if his skin was directly attached to his skeleton.

I checked his breath with my fingers, and felt no breath was coming out from his nose. Then I checked his pulse and the heartbeat. Those were so feeble that it seemed he was about to die soon.

I cancelled the journey, and brought him to my abode.

I employed the best royal physicians for his treatment. Finally, he got his consciousness back after staying unconscious for three days.

I was present there at the moment when he regained consciousness. He was lying on the bed like a dead body, and suddenly he sat up instantly on the bed within a blink of an eye.

His sudden awakening frightened me for a moment, as I had never seen a person like him who was about to die a few days ago, and now he was acting like nothing had happened to him. His spoken words surprised me more.

He said, "World is in danger. I need to stop him soon."

There was no thought of other danger that could have come to my mind except the demon, Kali.

I asked him surprisingly, "What danger are you talking about?"

"I don't want to tell you, because you are not going to believe like others, and most importantly, I don't want to receive the same punishment again from another king."

"No danger is able to agitate me more than the demon, Kali."

"Oho! What a surprise!" said the man, "Finally I found a person who has knowledge about Kali."

I was excited after hearing Kali's name from an unknown person. I asked him without wasting any moment, "How do you know about Kali? And how to stop him?"

"I am a sage, and I possess a few extra abilities that ordinary sages can't imagine. I can feel whether an object is holy, or an evil resides in it, simply touching it. During the past few years, I have been feeling that a dark evil is growing inside any metallic objects. At first, I could not understand what it was. Therefore, I used the ability of a very powerful yoga, and found that after the end of the previous three Yugas, Kali has arrived here to ruin the entire society, spreading his evil powers. As soon as I came to know about it, I preferred to inform about the upcoming danger to our king, Janmejya. It was a wrong decision. When I told him about it, he considered me as a mentally ill person, and after that, he exiled me from my motherland, Kuru. While I was travelling to find a new place, I became weak due to starvation for many days. One time, I fell on the road losing my consciousness. And now I find myself on this bed."

"My brother Janmejya did this to you? Very strange."

"Yes, Kali begins to corrupt everyone's mind, and soon the world is going to be a place of demons in human disguises."

"Is there any way to stop Kali?"

"Yes, there is a way."

"What is it? Let me know."

"Purification of those metals by fire. But collecting every metal piece is impossible."

At that moment, an idea blinked inside my mind. I asked, "If all the metal pieces are collected for a definite place, is it possible to keep the place pure from Kali's evil, purifying those pieces."

"Yes, it is possible," answered the man, after a long pause.

"I've collected all the metallic objects of my kingdom. Please save my kingdom from Kali's grasp."

The sage agreed to do that.

We lit fire at a secret place in this castle, and he started the ritual of purification process.

Several months passed, and the progress of the purification was very slow. In those days, he became my good friend. His name was Satvik, the forefather of Kaivartya.

In daytime, Satvik remained busy meditating himself, and after sunset, he performed the act of purification, until he went to sleep.

I thought, if he continued that way, it would take twenty to thirty years to purify all the metallic objects. The slow progress agonized me very much. I was losing my patience.

One day I asked him if there was any alternate way to destroy Kali.

He answered, "I need a deep meditation to find the answer. I will answer the question tomorrow, after the sunset."

The whole next day, I waited for his answer, and as usual, after the sunset, he opened his eyes, returning from the deep state of meditation.

"I asked him, "Did you find the answer?"

Satvik nodded, "Yes, there is an alternative way, but the act is seemingly impossible to perform."

I said to him in disappointment, "Still, let me know the procedure."

"You couldn't understand what I said. We are unable to proceed even with its first step. We have to find out the origin, and no one knows what was the origin."

"What is 'origin'?" I asked.

"The origin is that metal object where Kali had taken shelter in the beginning."

"I know which metal piece was the origin."

"You know? Then why didn't you tell me before?" asked Satvik.

"Because you haven't asked me earlier."

"Even if we find the origin piece, the next procedure is still going to be difficult."

"What do you have to do next?"

"We have to find the person who has given the permission to Kali to stay inside that metal piece. But due to the evil effect of Kali, the person is likely to be dead soon after that. Still we have to find another person of the same bloodline."

"My father, Parikshit was that person, and I am his son. Eventually, I am carrying his blood."

Then I described to him the past incident that had happened to my father.

He suggested that I should fetch that golden crown from Kuru.

I did not waste time. I went to Kuru, and met my brother, Janmejya after many years. And after a long conversation, I finally convinced him. He handed over the golden crown, and I came back to Dharmkhet.

I gave the crown to Satvik, but he did not touch the crown with his hand. Instead, he used a piece of cloth to hold, avoiding the direct contact to the metal.

He said, widening his eyes, "I can feel him inside. Oh! He is so powerful that I fear to imagine."

"Now tell me what to do next. How can I destroy the demon forever?"

"This is going to be the most difficult of the entire process. The heir of Parikshit who is going to destroy Kali, must be in his pure state."

"I couldn't understand what you've said."

"That person should have to be completely free from Kali's effect. If any evil part of Kali is residing inside him, he will die."

"I am completely free from his influence. I can definitely do it."

"If you believe so, you may proceed."

Satvik brought me near the fireplace, where the process of purification was going on.

I still remember that day when I died. Satvik had instructed me to stand in front of the fireplace, I was standing there holding the crown.

Satvik was chanting some powerful mantras, and along with the chanting I was feeling the hot radiation of the ignited fire on my face.

After a few hours, he said, "Now throw the crown into the fire."

I did so, but as soon as it touched the fire, it sprang out of the fireplace, and fell down on the floor.

At that moment, we heard the dreadful laugh of that demon. Doubtlessly, it was coming from the golden crown. My heart was pounding in fear, and at the next instant, the demon appeared in front of us, coming out from that crown.

Kali said, "What did you think, you are going to destroy me that way?"

We had nothing to do against him at that moment. We remained standing still at our own positions.

The demon continued, "You were not able to destroy me, because an evil part of mine resided inside you that you were not able to feel it, ha ha. You are not going to harm me anymore. I could have shown you mercy, but you and your people made me angry, and all of you deserve punishment from me. Perhaps your death can reduce my anger a bit. Before I kill you, I put a curse on the dwellers of Dharmkhet. From this moment, they are not able to touch any metals. Not only that, if any outsider comes to this land, he will also bear the same curse. If ever anyone touches any metals by mistake, he or she will transform into the same metal."

I remained immobile at my place. The demon had frightened me. Still I shouted at him, "I will protect my people forever, and I will not let them touch any metallic object."

Kali laughed again, "How can you protect them after your death? My evil force will make them greedy. Thus, everyone will be compelled to touch metals one day, forgetting about the severe danger."

"After my death, my soul will evacuate them from Dharmkhet. Your intention will never be successful."

"They cannot leave the place, as I built an invisible impenetrable wall surrounding the place. Forget about your people. Now it is the time for your death."

Suddenly, I felt a severe pain inside my chest, and I died.

*****

My death was not my end. I became a spirit, and vowed that I should be protecting my people from Kali's grasp.

Just after my death, Satvik did not lose hope. He performed a terrific penance for many days intending to summon Mahakaal, the god of time.

The penance was powerful. One day indeed the god appeared to him, and showed us a little hope.

Mahakaal said that one day a descendant of Parikshit would arrive at Dharmkhet, and he would be able to eliminate the curse. But the fire of that Yagna should not be extinguished, until the descendant of Parikshit would make everything normal.

Once I appeared to Satvik, and he informed me about the little hope, which had been shown by Mahakaal. And he promised me that his every heir would keep the fire ignited until the arrival of the heir of Parikshit at Dharmkhet. Moreover, his every heir would assist me with every manner.

Thereafter, Satvik married a girl, and his entire generations have been living in Dharmkhet for more than thousand years. And as a spirit, I have been keeping evil away from people's minds, punishing them for every sin.

Chapter Twenty-one

The crown

"You are the descendant of Parikshit, Aditya. Our destiny brought you here. You are that person, looking for whom, I was waiting for thousand years. You can save everyone in this land from the curse, and after that, I can achieve my liberation peacefully," said Vikranta.

Aditya sighed, "I used to be a scion of Kuru, but I lost that recognition due to a curse. Kuru does not belong to me anymore."

"I know all of it. Being a spirit, I possess a few abilities like to read a person's mind, or to know his past. I know, you are still carrying the same blood of Parikshit in your veins. And just think, that girl Mitra can live, and after that, you and Mitra will make a happy family together."

"If you believe I am that person, who can make everything normal, I shall do it. I shall do not only for that girl, but for everyone, and for society," said Aditya.

Vikranta smiled, "I expected that kind of answer from you. Your mind is now entirely free from the demon's grasp. You became a selfless person, which is quite opposite from your previous character."

"All those previous activities of mine were unfortunate. That evil demon lived inside me, and his evil power was responsible for all my past actions. I was unaware about him until he appeared before me. I met him twice. First time while I was going to enter Dharmkhet, he prevented me. And next time he appeared to me before leaving my body. He ruined my life, and he deserves a strong punishment. Please tell me how I can destroy that demon," said Aditya.

"Kaivartya will show you the right path," said Vikranta.

Then he said to Kaivartya, "You should know what to do. Take him to the Yagna (fireplace). I am coming shortly."

Kaivartya nodded briefly, and said, "Come with me Aditya."

At first, Kaivartya lit a torch detaching it from the nearby wall, and slowly moved along a wide corridor. Aditya followed him silently. That region of the castle was unknown to him, as he never came there. Countless metallic statues were stored in that corridor, and those were composed of different metals. Most of them were iron statues, and others were of copper, silver, or gold. Moreover, they were posing differently in their own facial expressions and gestures.

Aditya realized that they were unaware about the danger at the moment of transformation. Some were talking with others, some were busy in their daily work, some, and some were doing nothing, just had been transformed into metals because they had touched metals somehow.

Kaivartya spoke first to break the silence of the uncanny environment.

He said, "If Vikranta did not exist today, all of us would have been transformed into them."

"I'm really overwhelmed after listening to the entire story. He sacrificed his life for his people. It must have been a great sacrifice. I'm grateful to him too. If he did not treat me like that, Kali would live inside me forever."

"Yes, he has changed the characters of many people, and saved them from harm. Despite that, he failed to protect his own family. Look at those two statues. They used to be Vikranta's wife and son. At the moment when the curse had taken effect, they were in direct contact with metals."

Aditya observed those statues carefully. First one was the wife of Vikranta, who had been a pretty looking woman, and she was wearing several metallic ornaments in her neck, head, and hand. Aditya understood the reason why she had been transformed. And the second one was Vikranta's son, standing like a warrior carrying an open metallic sword in his hand.

Kaivatya halted near a large door at the end of the corridor.

He opened the gate with a gentle trust, and Aditya could see in the dim light of the flame torch that there was a staircase leading to the underground.

They slowly moved down through the staircase, and came to the hall where the fireplace was situated.

The underground hall was enormous. A king generally built such hidden halls in his castle to provide shelter for the civilians when another king attacked his land.

Aditya did not find any metallic statue there, but a large fireplace in the middle. It was called Yagna, where sacred rituals were performed by a king.

The Yagna was shaped like a large bowl, and it was made of marble. Several decorations were carved outside of it.

Aditya noticed, bundles of firewood were kept near the walls, and he understood at that moment where Kaivartya came carrying firewood, in every two or three days' gap.

For many years, he kept the fire ignited. His father had done the same, his forefather had done the same for a thousand years. No one in Dharmkhet knew about that secret.

On a concrete platform, the golden crown of Parikshit was placed. Kaivartya picked up the crown from its place touching it with his fingers.

"Why did you touch it?" shouted Aditya frighteningly.

"It is the only metallic thing that we can touch. The curse does not work for this particular metallic object, because it is the origin," clarified Kaivartya, "Now hold this, and stand near the Yagna. I'm going to start the process."

Kaivartya added a few more pieces of firewood into the Yagna to increase the strength. Aditya was standing still holding the crown, facing the fire. Meanwhile Vikranta appeared there to watch the ritual.

Kaivartya was chanting some Mantras, and along with that, sprinkling a liquid fuel into the fire. That liquid was creating an agitation in its flame.

After a certain period, the most awaited moment came. Kaivartya said, "Let the fire touch the origin."

Aditya obeyed his instruction fearlessly, throwing the crown into the Yagna.

An intolerable melancholic scream of Kali came out from the Yagna, and echoed around the hall. It seemed that the demon was suffering from extreme pain. And Aditya felt nothing. He just fell on the floor losing his consciousness.

Chapter Twenty-two

The hell

"Am I dead, or it's just a dream?" asked Aditya himself.

He found himself standing in an incredible place which could not be believed to exist on earth. The sky was covered with dark clouds, and a continuous rumbling sound persisted there, because lightning was occurring in every region of the sky.

The ground was covered with ashes instead of soil, and due to the presence of heavy wind, ashes created a haze around him.

Aditya looked around, but there was nothing except the horizon, no tree, no river, no sea, and no human or animal. It was just a combination of ashy ground and bad weather.

Aditya suddenly heard a voice from behind.

"Aditya, my son."

Aditya turned around shockingly, as he knew, there was no one in the world who could call him 'son' except his father. Indeed, the person was his father, Mahendra.

"Pitasree (father), you are here? What kind of place is this?" asked Aditya in astonishment.

"This is the abode of Kali. He lives here, and he keeps all of his prisoners who had failed to survive from his atrocious tricks."

"But I saw you in Kuru where you are still alive as an emperor."

"That was not me. Maybe that person and I look alike, but our souls are different."

"How is it possible?" asked Aditya.

"The universe is mysterious, Aditya. We believe there is only one universe where we live, and spend our entire life. But the truth is, there are too many just like an uncountable number of stars in the sky. Every universe is running in its own timeline and incidents. In a particular universe, you were born as my son, and in another, you do not even exist. But your soul is a constant entity. Every incident, which you have experienced in your life, was actually experienced through your soul. In my case, that king that you had seen in Kuru was another person, who was carrying a different soul than me, and was not your father. But here, Kali has confined my soul, and I am unable to achieve my liberation."

"As I know you, you were a good human being. How was Kali able to capture you here?"

"Becoming a good person is not enough to escape from the evil grasp of Kali. A good maintenance of my duties was also important. I failed to maintain it properly."

"How could it be? I observed that you performed your duty as a king in a flawless way. All dwellers of Kuru were too happy when you ruled the kingdom."

"I didn't fail as a king, but as a father. I failed to make you a good son. If I treated you well from your childhood, Kali would not be able to deviate your mind towards evil, and all those unfortunate incidents that you had to face in your life would not happen."

"Pitasree (father), I've learnt that every undesired incident happens in our life for overall good. If those events did not happen in my life, I would not come here to execute a wise mission."

"What is your mission, Aditya?"

"I've come here to destroy Kali forever. I have to kill him, and save those lives who have been living in their metallic form for more than a thousand years."

"I've been trying to defeat him too. But he is very powerful. Perhaps you are the person who is capable of defeating Kali. I can only wish good fortune for you, and provide a sword to fight."

Mahendra offered him the same sword that he received on his eighteenth birthday from his father.

"Pranaam Pitasree. Please bless upon me that I can achieve victory."

"My blessings are always with you, my son. Victory shall always be yours," said Mahendra, "Now I should go from here. I can't stay here with you for longer. Goodbye my son."

Mahendra disappeared from there, and Aditya looked around the place, carrying the open sword, to find Kali, intending for a duel against him, but found him nowhere.

"Where is Kali?" thought Aditya.

"I am here, Aditya. You don't have to find me. I am everywhere, because this place is mine."

Aditya found the demon in front of him. He was standing a few steps away.

He ran towards him, as soon as he found Kali.

Blistering burn marks were visible on his skin. In spite of that, it seemed, he did not lose his enthusiasm for a fight. Aditya was sure that the burn marks had resulted due to the Yagna, into which he had cast the golden crown.

"How dare you capture my father in your hell?" shouted Aditya Angrily.

"How dare you put me on fire?" yelled Kali with the same tone.

Both of them were in an equal aggression for combat. Kali raised his sword, as Aditya did the same.

Within a few moments, an incredible duel began between Kali and Aditya, and the rumbling of thunder sounded dimmer in presence of the sound of clanging swords.

They were equally powerful and violent. Whenever Aditya was attacking him applying his entire strength, Kali was doing the same, and whenever Aditya was stepping back to save himself from the strike of Kali's weapon, Kali was also doing the same.

The combat continued for hours, and it yielded no conclusion. After a certain period, Aditya felt tired, and he needed respite from the duel. Aditya glanced at Kali's face to observe his condition. He was looking tired.

Aditya stepped back a few steps from Kali to see whether he would do the same, or he would attack more aggressively, finding him weaker.

Interestingly, Kali did not attack back, instead he stepped back too, following Aditya's activity.

Aditya sat on the ashy ground to take some rest. Kali also did the same.

After a while, Aditya regained his strength, and stood up to fight again. Kali did the same action as usual.

Suddenly Aditya realized that Kali was imitating his every gesture. During the entire fight, Kali had moved his sword in the same direction that Aditya had moved. Aditya stretched his right leg forward to check the validity of his prediction, and surprisingly Kali copied his gesture. He stretched his left leg, and eventually Kali mimicked him again. Aditya made several gestures in front of Kali, and Kali perfectly followed every gesture.

An incredible idea illuminated in Aditya's mind at that moment. Finally, he found a way how Kali could be destroyed. If he would kill himself right at this moment, the demon would kill himself too. It might be the only possible way to finish him.

Aditya brought the sword near his throat, and gently touched it. Kali was standing at his place with the identical suicidal gesture.

Aditya was about to kill himself, meanwhile a voice echoed from the sky, "Stop Aditya. Do not end your life that way."

"This is the only possible way to destroy him. But who are you? Reveal your identity to me."

Lightning and thunder suddenly stopped, and the cloud departed for a certain region of the sky, making a portal. A magnificent beam of light came out from the portal, and shone the place removing the darkness.

The voice said, "I am Mahakaal, the creator and keeper of time, and maintains the balance of the entire universe."

Aditya knelt down, and bowed his head before the light.

The echoing voice continued, "You should not kill yourself aiming to kill the demon, Aditya. I created him for a purpose. His existence is necessary to keep the universe stable. If you kill the demon, the balance of the universe will be hampered."

"But an evil being cannot maintain a balance. Kali is evil, and he will destroy everything by poisoning people's minds."

"Sometimes destruction is good, and I created him for that particular purpose.

I created humans, and provided them knowledge and intellect, due to which they became unique, and beyond comparison with other animals. I created trees and plants, oceans and rivers, mountains, deserts, islands, and everything you see. I created these natural resources for all those creatures who are living on the earth. But humans think they are free to use anything infinitely. Presuming such a misconception, they have been consuming natural resources since their creation. They are destroying forests to increase the amount of inhabitable lands for living; they are polluting seas and rivers; they are digging mountains, and collecting materials to build their houses and roads; and they are applying several other methods to destroy my creation. That way they are inviting destruction of the world much earlier.

It is true that destruction of the world is inevitable. But humans are not allowed to alter its longevity. The world should have to be destroyed at the exact moment that I have predestined in the future. And after the destruction, I will recreate everything from the beginning. This is the way how the balance of nature is maintained.

Everything would happen in the predestined manner, if humans kept their population within its threshold limit. But day by day, they are increasing their numbers, thus they are infringing the balance, consuming more natural resources than I had estimated for them.

The balance should be maintained like before. And in order to maintain that, the human population should have to be decreased. The demon Kali has been created to accomplish that purpose. He lives in their minds, and produces several bad qualities among them. Those qualities made them violent. As an obvious effect, they do fight against each other, and it results in a deadly war. The war summons many deaths, and that way, the human population remains under the threshold, and accordingly, the balance of nature is sustained.

This is the reason why Kali exists. He plays an important role in society."

"Your explanation has eliminated my confusion indeed. It answered the question that I have been looking for. I always wondered why God had created evil besides his other beautiful creations. Now I came to know, evil too has a wise purpose.

Despite the explanation, I am concerned about the people of Dharmkhet. They have been suffering because of him. He had put a curse on them that they would not be able to touch any metals, and the curse transformed many innocent people into metallic statues. He also created an invisible wall around the village. The people live inside the village as prisoners for a thousand years. They are even not allowed to go anywhere leaving the village. And what about my father, and others who are staying in this hell? All their sufferings are seemingly not related to the balance. Why should people suffer without any reason? They should have lived their happy lives, but the demon has taken away their freedoms."

Mahakaal answered, "Everything is happening in this universe for a reason. Their sufferings are not any exception. Every sorrow or happiness is related to their souls. A soul must have to suffer for its sins that have been done in his past lives, or in the present. No one can escape from the inevitable truth.

Now I declare that from this moment, all their sufferings have gone, along with that, the curse has been also eliminated. Moreover, I am blessing a boon on the people of Dharmkhet that Kali will not be able to affect them. The place will remain free from any evil force throughout the future."

"And what about others? Many people like me want to stay away from him. But Kali has wished to corrupt everyone on the earth. It sounds alarming for the liberation of their souls."

"I do agree with what you have said. I have taken some of his powers away from him. He will not be able to apply his power on anyone until a person invites Kali. It means if the person continues to perform sinful acts knowingly, he will trigger Kali too. Thereafter, Kali will insist him to do more sin, and the person will become a slave of Kali. Apart from those people, he will not be able to harm anyone. Now it is the time for your return. You should go back to your own body."

Aditya observed the light had gone away, and Kali was not there. An ocean of darkness surrounded him suddenly. That instant change frightened him a bit, and the next moment, he felt the ashy surface, on which was standing, vanished.

He was falling down. He extended his limbs to find a support, but there was no support. He kept on falling down until he went back to his original body.

Chapter Twenty-three

Liberation of Vikranta

Aditya was awake, and found himself lying on a bed. He recognized the bed, and the room. He was at Daruk's home. On this bed he had found himself earlier, when he came to Dharmkhet for the first time, and he had to spend several months staying in this room.

He lifted his head a little, and saw a girl who was tidying up things inside the room. Aditya could not see her face, as the girl was facing the wall. Aditya anyhow wanted to see her, because for an unknown reason, he was subconsciously feeling a deep connection that was existing between him and her.

Aditya sat up on the bed, and gently spoke a word, "Hello."

The girl turned around, and Aditya became able to see her face.

He was stunned, and kept on gazing at her. It was her. The beautiful girl who had been merely a metallic statue, now was very alive, standing in front of him. She was more beautiful than he had seen in her sculptured form. He could not resist himself, but gazed at her.

"It seems you see me for the first time," said the girl.

"Do you know me?" asked Aditya.

"Of course I know you. You came to see me often when I used to be a gold statue, and you kept on staring like me this way."

Aditya was bewildered, and felt shy.

Meanwhile, Daruk entered the room smiling. He said, "Kaivartya told me that you're the person who has made everything normal. The curse has gone, and all metal statues came back to life."

"Mahakaal told me so," said Aditya thoughtfully.

"You've met Mahakaal? Is it real?"

"I think so. After a brief conversation with him, I was falling down. But I couldn't understand how I reached here. Maybe it was a dream."

"It was not a dream, Aditya. When Kaivartya brought you here, there was no sign of life in your body. I thought you were dead. But, Kaivartya told me that you were still alive, only your soul was outside of your body. Staying in that state for three days, you came back to life again," said Daruk.

"Is she your daughter, Mitra?"

Aditya already knew the answer, yet he asked the question to show formality, and he also wanted to know trivial things about her.

"Yes dear, she's my daughter, and she remains the same age that I've seen him for the last time. I'll introduce you to my wife too. But first of all, you have to go to the castle. Kaivartya told me that Vikranta wants to meet you for the last time. So, as soon as your consciousness returns, you should go there."

"Where is Vikranta going?" asked Aditya remorsefully.

"I don't have the answer. But you must go to the castle now, without wasting much time."

*****

Aditya arrived at the castle, and observed that the castle had a drastic change. Once it had been a place of dead statues, now they were alive. The entrance of the castle was guarded by royal guards, and inside was also crowded with people.

When Aditya entered the castle, everyone bowed down their heads showing him gratitude. Dharmkhet was now free from the evil grasp of Kali because of him.

Aditya looked at the throne. It was still empty.

Kaivartya was already present there. Aditya went to meet him, as soon as he could see him.

"You are here, that means Vikranta will appear soon. For the first time he is going to appear himself in front of everyone present here. Probably it is going to be his last appearance."

"Why last? Where is he going?"

"His soul will achieve its liberation, and can find a womb for rebirth."

"It means we can't see him again? He is leaving us forever?" asked Aditya.

"Exactly so. A soul becomes a ghost, because he failed to accomplish his unfinished task when he lived as a human. It's very painful. A soul should not deserve the life of a ghost. It is as painful as living the life of a prisoner for a lifetime. So a soul must achieve its liberation. Vikranta had to live as a ghost because the curse persisted. Now the curse has been eliminated, thus Vikranta peacefully renounces his ghostly body."

Meanwhile a royal guard announced loudly, "The queen of Dharmkhet, Maharani (queen) Minakshi, and her son, prince Vikram are approaching at the Hall."

"They are still alive!" whispered Aditya in astonishment.

"It sounds insane, but true. During the entire period, while they had been staying as metallic statues, their age remained unchanged. This fact is true for all the soldiers, royal guards, and other villagers who had touched metallic objects in the past. They all have come to life now," clarified Kaivartya.

The queen and the prince entered the hall, and they were looking gorgeous in their royal dresses and ornaments.

Within a few moments, Vikranta appeared, and the noise of people's chatting stopped suddenly as they could see the ghost before their eyes. Everyone bowed their heads before him.

They were looking for a speech from him. Without making them wait long, Vikranta began the speech, "Dear my fellows, about thousand years ago I used to be the king of Dharmkhet. It was indeed a long period of time, yet I hope you still remember me. I am Vikranta.

During these years, most of you existed as metallic statutes, and I was roaming around the place as a dissatisfied soul. It had happened due to an atrocious curse which remained intact for a thousand years. But now the curse has been eliminated, and it became possible because of Aditya. You got relief from your metallic bondage, and from now on, you are free to use metals without any fear.

As the curse has been eliminated, I deserve a long awaited peace of my soul. Soon I am going to achieve my liberation renouncing this spirited form. After that, I shall never appear before you again in the future.

For a thousand years, I continued ruling the place as a ghost of the dead king. But after my disappearance, Dharmkhet will need a new ruler. According to the old rule, my son, Vikram deserves the position. But he is only fifteen, and underage to be a King. So, I decided that Aditya should receive the responsibility as the king."

"I don't want to be a king," shouted Aditya, as soon as he could hear that his name had been declared for the position of the king of Dharmkhet.

"Why not, Aditya? I hope you would rule Dharmkhet in a perfect way," said Vikranta.

"It has several reasons. I can't explain those right at this moment. But I insist you, you should not consider me for the position of the king of Dharmkhet."

"Do you agree to rule the place until my son reaches his eighteen?"

Aditya thought for a moment and answered, "Yes, I do."

"Alright then, my son will sit on the throne, but he should have to rule Dharmkhet according to the decision taken by Aditya in every step. When he will reach his eighteen, he will receive the full power as a king."

"Long live the king. Long live the king," cheered the crowd.

Then Vikranta met his family for the last time, and Aditya noticed the queen and his son were crying while saying him goodbye.

At the moment of liberation, Vikranta's ghost form dissolved in air, and transformed into a flare, and it went away forever.

Many people were crying in sorrow, as they knew they will never able to see Vikranta again in the future. Aditya was sobbing too.

Everybody loved Vikranta after all.

Chapter Twenty-four

Happy life

Time flowed like a river.

After the disappearance of Vikranta from Dharmkhet, Aditya became the new ruler. During his span of ruling the kingdom, he ruled the kingdom so well that it became prosperous again like it had been before, when Kali had not yet affected the land. In those days, the son of Vikranta, Vikram gathered the idea of how to become a king, observing the techniques of how Aditya had been ruling the kingdom. Also, Aditya was preparing him as a future king, delivering him knowledge selflessly.

Three years later, Aditya handed over the responsibility of Dharmkhet to Vikram, according to the words that he had given to Vikranta. And after that, he got married with Daruk's daughter, Mitra, and made a happy family.

Two years after his marriage, Mitra gave birth to a son. Aditya chose a good name for him, Anant, the meaning of which was infinite.

As time went by, Anant grew up. Soon Anant would be eight years old. And that way, Aditya had spent more than fifteen years in Dharmkhet.

Adiya continued his farming business, and lived in Dharmkhet as a wealthy person. Despite having enough money, he liked to spend maximum of it for the welfare of poors, as poverty still existed among some people in Dharmkhet.

Overall, Aditya was leading a happy life there. He had a good wife, an adorable son, Kaivartya and Daruk as his guides, a good profession, and a good life. He got everything good in Dharmkhet.

Did he forget about his past life?

Once he used to be the prince of Kuru, and his father loved him very much. Had he forgotten his father's affection?

He had no answer to those questions, as he stopped asking himself such questions after a certain period, when he realized that he did not have the ability to compare both the lives side by side. Whenever he had a thought about his father, he began to think about his wife and son, as they deserved their own values near him just like his father. At this point of his life, he did not know which life deserved more value near him.

*****

It was the eighth birthday of Anant, and he was very happy as it was the day for a trip. Aditya brought his son under the same rosewood tree, on the top of the cliff, near the lake, where he used to come many years ago to find peace, and to get rid from the memories of those unfortunate events that had happened in his past life. That beautiful place had a magical ability to transform a person's mind from its remorseful state into happiness.

On that sunny afternoon, Aditya was sitting by Anant, under the rosewood tree. A gentle breeze was blowing from the northern mountain side. The weather was neither hot nor cold, and several birds were flying towards the south, indicating that winter was near.

Anant asked his father, "Pitasree, does a past life really exist?"

Aditya thought for a moment, and answered, "Of course past life exists. one year ago, you were seven years old, and throughout that year, you gathered many memories. Those memories were from your past life. Now you are living in your present life, and there are too many years left for your future life."

"I already know those things. I'm not talking about my past years. I'm talking about something else."

"What are you talking about, Anant?" asked Aditya, smiling.

"I am talking about a life before someone's birth. Can someone live another life before his birth?"

Aditya was surprised. Why was his son asking such a question at that age? Surely someone put that concept into his head, Aditya thought.

Aditya said, "Many people believe in the existence of that kind of life, and many people don't."

"What do you believe, Pitasree? Do you believe in past life?"

"I believe in many supernatural things that many people are not able to imagine. But why are you asking such a question today?" asked a surprised Aditya, bringing a fake smile on his face.

"Because I had a few memories from my past. Those memories are not related to my recent life."

"Really? Can you share your memories with me?" asked Aditya in curiosity.

"Why not father. I used to be a king in my past life, and I had a son. My wife died when my son was a little child."

"Then?"

"When my son reached his eighteen, on his birthday he asked for a gift from me that I should invade our adjacent kingdom, and conquer it. Then, my son and I fought the war together against that kingdom, and became the reason for many deaths. The son of the enemy king cursed us, and I died. Then a demon captured my soul into a hell-like place, and there I lived for two years."

"Do you remember your son's name?" asked Aditya thoughtfully.

"Yes, I remembered. His name was Aditya, just like your name."

Aditya's eyes were moistened. Anant noticed his father was crying. He asked, "What happened, Pitasree? Why are you crying?"

"Nothing, my son. I'm not crying. Maybe dust particles fell on my eyes. But, you should not think about your past for long. Past memories make a man weaker. If a person remains locked in his past, he will never be able to go forward in his life. So my son, just forget those memories considering, as those were merely illusions created by your mind."

"Maybe those were illusions," said Anant thoughtfully, and after a pause, he said, "Or maybe not."

"May I go to pick some flowers?" asked Anant, aiming his finger towards a shrub containing beautiful flowers.

"Hmm, go," said Aditya thoughtfully.

His dead father finally returned as his own son? What a beautiful miracle happened in his life. No one on this earth could claim today that he was a happier person than Aditya. He needed nothing more in his life. His life was complete, and he was going to love this life more than the life of that poor prince once called Aditya.

Suddenly Aditya could hear the scream of his son, "Help me, Pitasree."

Aditya looked around, and did not find his son around there.

"Where are you?" shouted Aditya worryingly.

"I am hanging from the cliff," answered Anant.

Aditya looked down from the top of the cliff, and saw Ananta was hanging there, holding a small tree which had grown at its side.

"Hold on, Anant. I'm coming shortly," said a nervous Aditya.

Aditya tore off a long tree branch from the rosewood tree, and went to Anant, carrying the branch.

He stretched the branch to Anant lying on the ground, and said, "Grab it tightly. I'm picking you up."

But the branch was too short to Anant's reach. Aditya stood up, and found a small stone platform at the face of the cliff. He jumped on it.

"Grab it now."

Anant did so.

Aditya applied his entire force to lift up the branch carrying Anant, and successfully landed him on a safe place with the help of that branch. But Aditya failed to maintain his own balance, and slipped from the stone platform.

"Pitasree!" cried Anant badly, as he saw his father was falling down from the cliff.

"I don't want to die so soon. I want to live many years with my family." said Aditya to himself.

Within a few moments, Aditya's body touched the ground. No one could stay alive after falling from that height.

Aditya was dead.

Chapter Twenty-five

Aditya was not dead

Aditya was not dead. There was even no pain in his body after falling from that height, instead he felt a softness on his back. He was lying on something very soft.

His eyes were still closed in the tremendous fear of death, but he was very sure that he was not dead. Just before his body could touch the ground, an unknown magical force transported him in a safe place.

Aditya took a deep breath to get a reconfirmation about his state of aliveness. Yes, he was very alive, as he could feel the inhaled air inside his chest. It contained a strong smell of a perfume of some kind. It had the same smell that he had forgotten many years ago.

Aditya put his finger on that surface, on which he was lying. It was not grass, or something else related to nature, but it was very expensive velvet, as he felt.

Aditya opened his eyes, and found himself lying on a bed inside a room. He looked at the walls, and found twenty portraits hanging there. And found another large drawing on the wall depicting the map of Kuru kingdom.

It cannot be. Where is his son, Anant? Where is the cliff, from which he had fallen? Where is Dharmkhet, where he lived? Where is his lovely wife, Mitra? Where is Daruk and Kaivartya?

He found himself in a place, which had been forgotten by him many years ago.

"Oh god, I don't want to return to my previous life again. Please take me there, where I was."

Aditya prayed to god many times, closing his eyes, but nothing happened. Everytime he opened his eyes and found himself inside that same room again and again.

Aditya was weeping like a baby. The curse was eliminated, and the elimination of that curse gave him more pain than the moment when it had taken effect.

He looked at the mirror on the table to see his face, and found himself younger. At least fifteen years younger than he had been in Dharmkhet.

How could he get back that cursed life again? Aditya asked himself, but found no possible way.

He remembered, Vikarna's soul had said that the curse would be gone when he found the cursed life more precious than the original one. Now he realized how precious the cursed life was.

Suddenly he could hear the sound of approaching footsteps outside the room. It stopped near the entrance door, and a man's voice said, "The emperor of Kuru, the great Mahendra, wants to meet you, your royal highness. He's waiting for your consent to enter."

It sounded like a deja vu to him. It had happened many years ago when he had been just eighteen years old. It was happening again.

Aditya wiped his tears, and opened the door. He saw his father standing there, smiling at him.

"Happy birthday my son," said the king.

Aditya wanted to bring a fake smile on his face, but it did not come. A deep pain of losing everything was acting inside his heart.

"What happened to you, Aditya? It seems you're not happy today? Do you forget, it's your eighteenth birthday?" said Mahendra worryingly.

"I.... I.... I do not belong to this place. I am from somewhere else."

"Are you feeling sick? Is everything alright? Let me check your fever," said Mahendra.

Mahendra touched his fingers on his forehead, and found nothing to worry.

He said, "Your body temperature is normal. There is nothing to worry about. Still you're talking abnormally. Please tell me dear what happened to you. See, I brought a gift on your birthday."

Mahendra revealed a sword to him. Aditya had seen the sword before. It was the same sword, with which he had fought the war against Anga, and a duel against Kali.

"I belong to Dharmkhet. I want to go back there. A few moments ago I was there," said Aditya with a stagnant expression.

"Oh my dear, you must have seen a nightmare then. Just forget about it."

"It was not a dream. I was in Dharmkhet in reality. I've spent fifteen years of my life in Dharmkhet," muttered Aditya.

"I never heard the name of that place. Where is it? It was nothing but a dream. You've always been here all the time since your childhood."

"I'm showing the location of Dharmkhet on the map. It was...."

Aditya was stunned again.

"Where is Anga?"

"What happened to you today, Aditya? Don't you know, Anga doesn't exist today, because one of our forefathers had conquered that land many years ago. Every part of it belongs to our kingdom now."

Aditya saw a full picture of that sparrow on the map.

He was unable to bear further. He ran off from the room, as fast as he could, and took out a good horse from the stable, and set out for a journey towards Dharmkhet.

*****

His horse was running through the same road, through which he had entered Dharmkhet for the first time. He found the pond where he had taken a bath before arriving there. He realized Dharmkhet was near, and he was excited.

After travelling the required distance, he found the lake, the river, the mountains, those beautiful flowers on the lake, the waterfall, and other natural beauties nearby, but there was no trace of Dharmkhet. It was just a barren land where no one ever lived.

Aditya dismounted from the horse, and knelt down on the ground, putting his palm on his forehead, staring downwards. Tears flowed down from his eyes. He was crying in deep pain of losing everything for the second time.

"Why are you crying Aditya? The curse is eliminated, and you get back everything that you lost fifteen years ago. Isn't it a happy moment for you?"

A voice talked to him from behind. He recognized the voice. It was Vikarna.

Aditya turned around, and said, "I lost everything again. Please send me back to that cursed life. It was better than this life as a prince."

"It is not possible now. You are dead there. I can see your dead body lying on the ground, at the bottom of the cliff, and your wife, son, and other people are crying there. If you could keep yourself alive, I would try," said Vikarna.

"But I know that my son, Anant, is carrying the soul of my true father. That person in the castle isn't my father, whom I knew."

"A soul cannot be true or false. Every soul is important in someone's life. Just think, a few years ago you didn't know your wife, Mitra, or your son, Anant, but now they are valuable entities near you. From now on, if you consider that person as your father by your heart, he will become valuable again in your life."

"But how can I meet my son and wife again? They were everything for me."

"Not possible in your present life. They are still living in their own world in another universe. Maybe you will be able to meet them again in your next life, if you feel that a strong bond still exists between you and them," said Vikarna, "Now it is the moment of liberation of my soul. It deserves its liberation, because your curse has been eliminated at the end. Goodbye forever, Aditya."

Vikarna disappeared from there, after transforming himself into a beam of light.

Aditya stood up, and mounted on the horse, and led the horse towards Kuru.

It was time for returning to his own castle. Before returning, for the last time, he turned around, and beheld the entire place. Too many memories were still persisting in his mind regarding Dharmkhet. He looked at the land where Kaivartya lived; now there was nothing but a few bushes here and there. He looked at the land, where the castle of Vikranta existed; now the land was covered with a few boulders. He looked at the place where he once lived; now it was covered with trees and plants.

Aditya sighed, and a few drops of tears came out from his eyes, and they dropped on the ground. He would not ever be able to see Anant and Mitra again. Yet, they would remain forever only in his memory.

Aditya ran the horse towards Kuru, leaving behind the blowing sands.

The End

Other books by this author: